Illegal Love

FELICIA TRUTTIER

authorHOUSE®

AuthorHouse™
1663 Liberty Drive
Bloomington, IN 47403
www.authorhouse.com
Phone: 1-800-839-8640

© 2010 Felicia Truttier. All rights reserved.

No part of this book may be reproduced, stored in a retrieval system, or
transmitted by any means without the written permission of the author.

First published by AuthorHouse 5/20/2010

ISBN: 978-1-4520-1024-3 (e)
ISBN: 978-1-4520-1023-6 (sc)

Library of Congress Control Number: 2010905107

Printed in the United States of America
Bloomington, Indiana

This book is printed on acid-free paper.

Front Cover Image by Kendall Putmon
Back Cover Image by John Johnson

Dedication

The dedication of this book goes to all the people that believed in me even when I did not believe in myself.

First giving thanks to **GOD** for whom I would not be here today.

Then to my family:

Helen Little   **Elaine Broughton**
Valencia Broughton   **Shontella Evans**
Alexis Doye   **Robin Greene**
Ruth Johnson
(My kids, Ariel, Nicole, Chelsea, Derrick, Ali & Mark)

To the many friends that read the original version and even with all the errors loved the story line.

Linda Meade   **Nikki Brooks**
Clarence Maddox   **Niyokia Partridge**
Sharon Fraiser-Hagan **Karen Johnson**

A special thanks to **Francine Pond** for correcting so many mistakes on my original draft.

To *Reginald C. Moore* who stood by me even through the toughest of times.

In addition, to my father who would have been one of my biggest fans **Theodrick Broughton**

God is good all the time
And all the time *God* is good.

A special thanks to a church that teaches me that God is good. ***Church In The Now*** with ***Bishop Jim Earl Swilley***.

Thanks to **Alanna Boutin** for the final editing and making my vision readable.

Acknowledgment

This book is a work of fiction. Sometimes names from everyday life are used. All characters are a product of the author's imagination. Any resemblance to actual events or locales or persons living or dead is purely coincidental.

This book is the pure thoughts and feelings of the author and no portion has come from any previous readings.

I am currently working on another novel if you are interested you may e-mail me at Felicia_truttier@yahoo.com

The Meeting

Why did I wear this easy-to-get-out-of dress? What was I thinking? Makeup? Why am I even wearing makeup? You would have thought that I was going somewhere to impress someone, but I'm not. As far as I'm concerned, I'm on my way to hell. As I walked up the stairs, the two flights seemed like the longest two flights I've ever had to take. With each step, I thought that my legs would give out on me, but maybe that was just a dream. Finally, I got to the door. He had said that when I got to the second floor, it would be the first apartment to my left, #221. Standing in front of the door, I had hoped that it was the wrong apartment door, complex or better yet—city.

Hesitatingly, I knocked instead of ringing the doorbell. He didn't come right away. I believe he wanted to make me suffer. I knocked again, my heart beating fast, maybe from the stair climb, maybe just knowing what was about to happen. When he didn't come right away, I hoped that I really had come to the wrong place. Just then, the door opened and there he was, standing in front of me in a blue silk house jacket and black pants. Tall, dark, bald-headed, white teeth and a beautiful smile. An anaconda smile. I didn't want to notice all of that, but I had no choice. There he was standing in front of me—my worst nightmare.

"Glad to see that you're on time," he said as I came through the door.

I didn't reply. Straight ahead of me, I saw the bedroom door. Brushing past him, I made my way to it. I could feel his eyes following me to the bedroom. I heard the door close behind me. It sounded like

ix

a great vault door slamming shut. I could sense him walking towards me, staring me up and down, probably sizing me up because he hadn't seen me in a while. I had already begun to unbutton my dress, and by the time he reached me, I just let it fall to the floor. I stood there with my back towards him, waiting. The chilliness of the room caused me to shiver a little. I knew that if he saw what the coldness had done to my breasts, it would excite him, and he would believe that it happened because of him. I lifted my arms to cover my protruding nipples. I didn't turn around as he came to my ear and whispered, "You know you don't have to do this; you can just walk away from all of this—from him."

I turned around angrily, looking him straight in the eyes. "Let's get this over with; I have somewhere to go!"

He took his hands and rubbed them over my shoulders as if to imply that he still had control over me. I kept my arms up as he lifted my slip off my shoulder. I felt nauseous. *I can't do this.* The slip slid down to the floor. He was just standing there behind me looking as I stood in front of him, completely naked. I could feel his stare. It had been a long time since I had seen him, but I knew him—oh, yes, I remembered him like it was yesterday.

"Are you sure?"

Without blinking or flinching, I turned around and replied to his question. "Let's get on with this so I can make my appointment."

He grabbed my head and kissed me hard. He was like fire, and I was like ice. I tried not to kiss him back, but it was hard. His soft brown mouth felt smooth and wet over mine. I had forgotten how good of a kisser he was until now. The taste of him was wonderful. It was clean, with a mixture of red wine. I thought that I would get intoxicated just from the taste of him. He stopped when he realized that I was not going to kiss him back.

He stepped back and looked at me up and down, then said, "I hope the rest of the evening isn't going to be like this, because if it is, then all bets are off."

"All you said was that I had to be here—in your bed—tonight. You didn't say that I had to participate. You just said I had to be here."

He picked up my things and threw them back at me. "Look, Nikki, if you are still into playing games, then go home. I don't need it."

By this time, I was getting aggravated. "Games!? This is what *you* wanted—not me, and by the way, I was *not* the one playing games. I believe *you* did that all by yourself."

He looked at me strangely, seeing the difference in me compared to before, I suppose. The old Nikki would never have spoken back to him. No, the old Nikki would have just lain down and taken it.

"Yeah, but the secret is yours."

"No, Anthony, the secret is *ours,* and we *both* have the same thing to lose."

With a confident smirk on his face he said, "Yeah, but eventually, I could win my way back. What about you? Do you think your fiancé will take you back after knowing you slept with his brother?"

Just hearing him say that made me want to cry, but I knew from experience with him that it would only make things worse. I dropped my things and grabbed his face. I kissed him, hard. I thought of Robert. I told myself that I could get through this evening if I could just pretend he was his brother. It shouldn't be hard; with only a year and a half difference between them, they almost looked like twins. When I stopped, he was happy. I could tell from his look.

"Now *that's* what I'm talking about. I think you need something to drink."

I hesitated for a moment but decided to take him up on his offer. "Yes, I guess you're right."

With a deep sigh, I sat on the bed and awaited his return, wanting to cry but knowing it would do me no good. I just sat there waiting for the inevitable. *Why was he doing this to me?* I didn't believe for one moment that he really loved me and wanted me back. It must be to hurt Robert.

I looked around. Everything looked so nice and new. It wasn't at all like the place we used to live in. It looked like he had moved up in the world, but I shouldn't be shocked. He had a way of getting what he wanted. Everything was neat and in its place. Everything seemed to be in order, but underneath, I knew the truth. You could hide some things from some people, but not from the people who knew you best—and I knew him. I guess I knew him as well as he used to know me. He finally came back with my drink. I quickly downed it and asked for another one.

"Do you think that's a good idea, Nikki?"

"I want another drink!"

The second one didn't go down as smooth, but it did go down. Then I demanded another. He probably could not believe his eyes, because I had never been a drinker.

xi

"You don't have to get drunk."

"Don't tell me what I have to do," I snapped.

He went to get the third drink, and by now, my brain was not functioning. He brought me the glass, and I could barely reach for it. I heard myself giggle.

"Girl, you're gonna be messed up."

I gave him a mean look. "What do you care?"

"You're right. It might be a little better, and I might get my old Nikki back."

I looked at him with drunken disgust. When I finished, he took my glass away. I sat there in my stupor, trying to make sense of it all.

He laid me down on the bed and then rolled me over. I felt the lights go dim. I told myself that I was not going to make this a pleasurable time for him, but then I felt a warm liquid on my back. He was putting massage oil on me, and then he started rubbing it in. I tried to resist and stiffen myself up, but it felt wonderful. Up and down my body. I felt his warm hands caressing every tender spot he could think of. I had been so tense since I had gotten the telephone call from him, but this, well; this was taking care of all of that. I started talking. I'm not sure what prompted it, but I started talking about all kinds of stuff, and he said he agreed or disagreed every now and then. Suddenly he stopped and told me to turn over. Every muscle in my body tensed back up again.

"Relax, just relax. I'm not going to do anything until I know that you're ready."

I was feeling a little woozy from the wine and said with a giggle, "Well, I might as well go home now."

I started to get up, and he softly pushed me back to the bed and whispered, "Just relax, girl."

He started the massage again from the bottom of my feet. I think that helped a little. It was ticklish at first, but once he had them relaxed, he continued up to my ankles and then my calves. It was all feeling so wonderful, I found myself getting angry because I was enjoying it so much. When he got to my thighs, I got scared again, but as he massaged me, I loosened back up. With one hand, he ran his fingers over the hairs that ran up to my navel, and with the other, he massaged the inner part of my thigh. I was getting afraid, but the wine loosened me up. Then he massaged between my legs. I didn't want to enjoy it, but I had no other choice. He was making me feel good. I felt trapped. He kept on massaging me, and then he leaned over and put his mouth on my breast.

xii

I could have exploded just from the initial touch. I gasped from the pleasure and breathed out his name "Noel."

He smiled, knowing that he had made me do this. Slowly he lifted his head up and said, "Shush, I won't do anything until you're ready."

Then he went back to kissing my breast. This continued for a while until I couldn't take it anymore. I screamed, "I'm ready!"

He stopped. With a contented grin on his face, he raised himself up over me and took off his robe. I remembered that beautiful body. Solid, muscular, beautifully browned. He should have been a model instead of a con artist. I remembered how passionate our lovemaking had been before and would now be again. I reached up for him. He lowered himself slowly to me, then put his hot mouth on top of mine. This time I responded. It was so wonderful. My head was swimming from the wine, but I believed everything would be all right in a matter of moments. He stopped kissing me and lifted himself up again. As he hovered over me, his look made me feel wanted. He went back to kissing one breast and then the other. He knew what made me desire him. He did not hesitate to use it against me. I had forgotten how good he was at what he did, but it was all coming back to me. He slid his tongue down to my navel and back up again, and for a moment, I thought I was losing my mind. *How could I be feeling such passion for this man?*

He asked if I was ready.

"Yes."

I was ashamed of myself, but I wanted him badly by now. Then he inserted himself inside of me and together our bodies rocked slowly up and down. We went from side to side and around back and forth, again and again. It was as if we had never been apart. Our bodies listened to each other and knew when to move. I raised my leg up high and laid it on his shoulder. He turned and put his teeth into my flesh. My leg ached, but it felt so good. Oh, the pleasure was too much. I screamed, "Robert! Robert!" He stopped in mid motion. I looked at him, not sure of what was happening.

"What's the matter? Why did you stop?"

"You called me Robert."

"I did not call you Robert."

He rolled off me. "Yeah, you did."

I just lay there trying to remember if I had actually said it. "I'm sorry, but what did you think? Did you think that tonight I would stop thinking about him?"

He said, "Well, no, you are my brother's woman now."

I tried to explain that I didn't know that they were brothers, but he just scooted to the edge of the bed and sat there with his head in his hands. I could tell that things were not going at all the way he had planned. I continued to lie in the same spot. I was afraid to move and afraid not to. I still remembered the things he had done to me before and knew that at any moment, he might go back to that person that had hurt me. In a very dry tone he said, "Go home."

I lay there for another minute, still afraid to move. I wanted to ask what he was going to do. I needed to know if he was going to tell Robert about us, but he said nothing, just staring into space. Then he got up off the bed and left the room. After a moment, I got up and gathered my things. I was trying to hurry but didn't want to leave anything. I didn't want any evidence left, showing that I had been here with him. As I walked out the door, I saw him sitting on the sofa in the living room. I could not leave without knowing what his intentions were. I was so nervous. I stood at the door looking at him.

"What are you going to do, Noel? I did what you asked. Are you going to tell Robert?"

He didn't look my way. He just said, "Nikki, leave now, or you'll be sorry."

As fast as I could, I ran down the same two flights that I struggled to climb earlier. When I got to my car, I was shaking so badly I could barely open the door. The keys felt like they didn't want to go into the lock. I took one last look up at the apartment I had just left and saw that he had turned the lights off. My heart was beating so fast. I sped out of the parking lot. As I drove towards my home, I couldn't control the tears that swelled up in my eyes. And then they began to cascade down my cheeks as it began to rain outside. *Now what should I do?* He still had the upper hand, and I wasn't sure how he would play it. I had to pull the car over because I couldn't see. The tears had me blind, and the rain didn't help at all. I just sat there for what seemed like forever, remembering what had gotten me into this mess in the first place.

Remembering: The Beginning

My life seemed to be going in all the right directions. I was starting a new job, and I was one year out of being in an abusive relationship. After taking some general computer classes at one of the local McDonalds to better myself, I would start a temporary job for a little law firm on Monday as a receptionist.

When Monday came, I was so nervous. It had been a long year, and this was the first job I had gotten in a long while that did not require me to wear a uniform that had my name stitched on it. When I got off the elevator, I was a little intimidated. I was led to believe that it was a small law firm, but what I saw made me think that it wasn't as small as the agency thought it was. As I stepped out of the elevator, I entered a very beautiful open lounge area with four leather love seats and plants all around. The blue furniture worked well with the off-white walls and the florescent lighting. It gave the office a sort of mellow atmosphere that was relaxing and subtle. You could tell that a service did the plants. They were everywhere and so nice, they almost seemed artificial.

Straight ahead of me was a woman sitting at the front desk. With a big smile, she said, "Hello, may I help you?"

"Yes, my name is Nikki Salime, and I was sent here by The Right Person Temp Agency."

The smile got larger as she stood up and extended her hand for me to shake. She introduced herself as Karan Timperman, the office manager. She was tall, about 5'10, and had a medium-brown complexion with short, light-brown hair. Her eyes looked hazel, and she had a nice smile, but she was not very attractive. An air of vanity radiated from the office manager. I knew that she thought a lot of herself.

She adjusted her clothes and came around to the front of the desk. I felt a little nervous about my attire when I saw how professional she was dressed. Although I didn't have much money, I tried to dress as businesslike as I could. Karan almost wiped her hands after the handshake, and the look she gave me was as if a prostitute had come to meet the women's auxiliary board at church.

"I'm so glad that you're finally here, and I can give this all to you." She laughed as she said this, then motioned me to go around to the side of the desk were she had been.

As I walked around the desk, the telephone lines lit up. She motioned me stay where I was as she went quickly around the desk to answer each call. She put them on hold or sent them to voicemail one by one until the phones stopped ringing. Then she went back to answer the first held call and then all the subsequent ones. She either took a message or transferred them to the extension of the person they were looking for. I was immediately impressed and hoped that I could live up to what they needed. Once she cleared the lines, she told me that she put the telephones on night ring. She said, "Only do this if you have to or whenever you leave the desk."

I nodded my head in agreement. Karan then took me around immediately to introduce me to all the associates. She said, "It will help you to know them all by face and to get to know where all of their offices are. You'll be expected to deliver their mail to them every day."

Again, I nodded my head in response. She stopped on the way down the hall to the first office and said, "I hope that you are not shy. These guys will eat you up if you are, especially Joel Blackwell."

"No, I'm not really shy. It will just take a little time to get used to everyone."

She replied, "Good."

Then we proceeded to the offices. There were five lawyers, all black. First, there was Thomas Chaney. He was short and stubby, not very attractive, and he had a stutter, but he seemed sweet. His office was the last one on the left side of the building. Second, was George Thimberton. He looked like he used to play professional football and was all buffed up. Even in his suit, I could tell he was bulging with muscles. His office was in the middle. Third, was Robert Jackson. He

xvi

looked sweet, innocent and gorgeous. Somehow, he looked familiar, too, and I hoped that he didn't think me strange by the way that I stared at him. His office was the first one and was closest to my desk and the closest one to the break room.

Then Karan took me to the break room and said, "Sometimes the guys bring stuff and leave it in the fridge. Don't worry, they each put their names on anything they bring, or they attach a note saying it belongs to the office, and, obviously, this means anyone can have some.

"Oh, yeah," she continued, "don't worry about having to clean up anything. We have a service that comes in and cleans each night."

I wanted to say cool but thought it was best just to shut up and listen. If they liked me, I would get to stay and experience everything they had to offer later. We went to the other side of the building where Karan introduced me to everyone there. We started from the first office this time. It was Kyle's. He was very attractive, tall, mocha-brown, clean-shaven, and wore a beautiful smile. I felt he was getting fresh already.

"Always a ladies' man," Karan said out of the corner of her mouth.

So far, Kyle's office was the biggest one. It took up the whole side of that building. I thought he must make the most money. Then there was Joel. He looked like he was quiet, but I could tell that he was sneaky. I wasn't sure if I could trust him. He reminded me of my ex-boyfriend, Anthony, except he was short and balding. Joel's skin was bad, and he an attitude that matched. My ex would act as if everything was fine and then from out of nowhere, he would just start punching me for no reason. I still had scars and nightmares from it. Joel's office was across from Kyle's, and it was the last room on that side. Next, we went to the conference room. It was huge, with a long mahogany table centered in it and eight leather chairs neatly tucked in. In the back stood a television set beside another long table.

"In here, we have all of the office meetings. That table in the back is where you'll put their lunch during those meetings, then you leave."

This time I did say it. "Wow."

She looked at me and giggled.

"I've never worked in a place like this before," I exclaimed.

"Oh, it isn't so much," she said as she lifted her eyebrow and showed me to the next room.

xvii

On the opposite side of the hall was her office. She then showed me to my desk and all the telephone lines. She showed me how to transfer the calls to everyone and explained how to sort the mail when it came in. As I settled down in my newly acquired seat, I looked at my surroundings and thought to myself, *I surely have come a long way.* My first couple of days went by fine.

Chapter 1

The following week started and everything was still good. I made several little mistakes but nothing serious. While sitting at my desk and sorting the mail, Mr. Kyle, as I secretly called him when no one could hear me, came leaning over my desk. I looked up and smiled. With his gorgeous smile gleaming down at me, he said, "Hi."

"Mr. Simmons, is there something I can help you with?"

"No, I just thought I'd stop by and ask you to stop calling me Mr. Simmons. Just call me Kyle like everyone else does."

I blushed a little. "Yes, sir."

"And what's with this 'sir' mess?" he said with a stern voice. "Are the other associates making you call them 'mister'?"

"Oh, no, I just haven't gotten used to everyone yet."

"Well, I insist on you calling me by my first name, and if you don't, then there will be severe punishments administered."

I smiled. "I'll try."

"Good, now that we have that out of the way, would you like to go to lunch with me?"

"If I say no, will there be severe punishments?" I asked as I tried to look up at him without blushing.

"Yes, of course there will be," he said as he gave me a little wink.

"Sure, I'd love to have lunch with you."

He told me that he would be back around 12:00 or 12:30, and I told him that would be fine.

Around 11:30, Karan came by and asked me what I was doing for lunch, and I told her that Kyle had invited me to join him. She said,

1

"Girl, I forgot to warn you about him. I need to give you the scoop on all of them, for that matter."

We went to the restroom down the hall, where she proceeded to tell me all about them. "Now, here's the deal. Tom is married, and he would be too scared to ask you out anyway. Women easily intimidate him, and when he gets nervous, he stutters a lot. He is an all right lawyer, and somehow, he makes it through the trials without stuttering. George is just a big loveable bear, but he's with Buffy. She is very prissy and very protective, and she hardly ever lets him out of her sight. Oh, but don't get me wrong. He might try something with you, but so far, he hasn't tried anything with any of the other girls that have worked here. Robert is so sweet and good-looking, but he has just come out of a bad relationship, and he was very unavailable while it was going on. By the way, he is a great lawyer, if not better, at least as good as Joel. No one really likes him, but he's Kyle's right-hand man."

"Kyle is the boss?"

"Yeah, but he doesn't like to boast."

Then she continued, "Joel is sneaky; he got the last receptionist fired, so watch out for him. He sometimes makes up tales to fit the situation, and on top of that, if Joel doesn't like you, then Kyle might not. Last but definitely not the very least is Kyle Simmons. He is wealthy, married, a damn good lawyer, damn good-looking, and he gets more ass around here than all of us put together. It's best to keep your distance from him, if you can, but he is very persistent. And one more thing, he won't hold the job over your head if you say no."

Karan said this with a sneaky grin on her face as she turned to walk away. She had suddenly made me very nervous. Here I was, the first week on the job, and I was going out to lunch with the boss. I didn't think that would look too good. Nervously I said, "Wait, Karan, I've already accepted a lunch date with him."

"That's not what I am telling you to say no to."

"Okay, I understand."

"I hope so, because believe me, he will try you."

We left the bathroom and walking back to my desk, I suddenly felt ashamed about my first opinion of her. She seemed like she was going to be easy to work with. I thought that she could help me not make any bad mistakes with the associates around here and possibly, when I get on my feet, she could help me with my wardrobe.

Kyle came shortly after my little class and asked if I was ready for lunch.

"Yes."

We left the office and went to the parking garage, where Kyle's 2003 Mercedes CL500 was parked. It was black with tinted windows and some very nice rims on it. Walking up to it, I thought it was as handsome as the owner was. Kyle was very nice; he even opened the door for me. I had never been in a car this nice before. The seats seemed to contour to my body perfectly. *What a life he must live.* The interior of the car was charcoal and the trim was like walnut burl. The car drove as well as I thought the owner might make love.

We talked as Kyle drove to the restaurant. He asked me questions about myself, and I answered as little as I possibly could. Lunch was in a very nice hotel. In the back of my mind, I kept thinking, was he trying to give me a hint? He never mentioned anything even remotely close to going upstairs, but I kept my guard up, waiting for a hint that we "take a look at a studio" that he keeps upstairs or something, but he never did.

Lunch was wonderful, and the food was excellent. I let him order for me. I was afraid to pick something too expensive, although he said I could have anything I wanted. During lunch, he mostly wanted to hear about me, but there wasn't much to tell, so we just talked about the office. We came back to the office late, and he told me not to worry about it. He would talk with my boss. I smiled and thanked him for everything. Of course, the first thing that happened when I got back was Karan motioning me to the restroom. I slipped back there with her, and she, of course, wanted to know everything. I told her what happened.

"Well, maybe he's just feeling you out a bit. When he gets his mind made up, he usually moves in real quick."

I told her that I would keep my guard up, then we went back into the office. The day was uneventful. All the associates were in and out all day, so I really didn't get to talk with anyone except for Karan every now and again. I went home feeling that everything was going right with this new job and my new life.

Work the next day was a little busier. The firm had a big case, and everyone had to help with it. I was sitting at my desk and noticed how tense most of the guys were regarding this case. Karan came in and said that the big deal was about a guy named Patrick Giddeons. He was

4 | *Felicia Truttier*

someone they deal with all the time, and he was always getting into some kind of trouble.

"Most of the guys want to drop him as a client, but he has a lot of money, and Kyle says that he needs representation anyway, and that they were as good a place for him to spend it on as any firm."

She stopped talking because Robert walked into the area.

"I'm waiting on a very important package, and when it gets here, please bring it straight to my desk."

"Yes sir."

"You don't have to say that to me."

"Oh, I'm sorry, I forgot."

He smiled, giving me a boyish grin that I thought probably gave all the girls goose bumps in high school.

"You'll be all right once you get used to all the cursing and screaming that goes on around here," he said.

My eyes got as big as saucers as I tried to imagine it. He must have realized I was trying to picture it because he said, "Nikki, that was a joke."

"Oh, I'm sorry."

He just turned and walked away. The office was busy all day with people in and out. The telephones were no better, calls all day. This was definitely *not* just a small firm. By the end of the day, I was beat. I had been answering, "The Peoples Law Firm," all day, and it was ringing in my head.

As I got into the elevator, Robert, Joel, and Kyle got in with me. All these nice, good-looking men, and I really didn't want one, nor could I have any one of them. They were talking about an upcoming case, and I couldn't relate, so I tuned them out. Then I heard Kyle say, "Isn't that right, Nikki?"

I jerked back to reality.

"What? I'm sorry, I wasn't paying attention."

Sarcastically Kyle said, "You weren't paying attention? Guys, this is just what I was saying. When a beautiful woman stops listening to you, there is *definitely* a problem."

"Oh, no, I was just trying not to eavesdrop. I didn't want anyone thinking I was listening to your business."

Then Joel said, "*Our* business is *your* business."

I looked down at the floor and hoped the doors would open soon. Kyle continued, "I like that she doesn't want to overstep her boundaries, but she knows when she needs to pay attention, isn't that right, Nikki?"

I looked back up, and he gave me a wink. I peeked over at Robert, who was looking up at the ceiling with a much-uninvolved look on his face. I felt that he was on my side also, but that Kyle came to the rescue before he could get there. My floor finally came, and I said good night to everyone.

I went outside to wait at the bus stop. While standing there, I saw Robert drive by. He honked, and I waved. He was in a fancy 2008 BMW 3 Series convertible 328i, green with a slight green tint on the windows. It was very classy. Next came Joel. He was driving out of the parking lot in an old, ugly, Ford LTD. It wasn't even clean. I wondered why he was driving such an old and ugly car. Then I realized it matched the personality that Karan had described. Finally, out came Kyle, but this time he was driving a Jaguar S-Type. He saw me, beeped and stopped.

"Do you need a ride home?"

"Oh, no, I'm fine. I always take the bus."

"Girl, come on, let me give you a ride."

I didn't want to seem ungrateful, so I just got into the car.

"Where do you live?"

I gave him the address. He said that he knew the area because he had grown up there.

"Really? Net you?"

"Yeah, me. I lived not two blocks from the apartments that you live in."

"You don't look like you come from a neighborhood like that."

He said, "Well, first of all, I wasn't born with a silver spoon in my mouth, and second, the entire neighborhood wasn't that bad when I lived there."

He told me that his father was a schoolteacher and his mother worked in the cafeteria of the elementary school that he attended. Then his father became a principal at one of the elementary schools, so they moved. Once the money got better, his mother went back to school to become a dietician. She was the head dietician for the school district in the East County until her death. A drunk driver had killed both his parents.

"Your parents sound wonderful. You must really be proud of them," Nikki said.

"Yes, I am. They are my parents, and I love them both dearly. What about you? You said that you were from here, but you didn't say what part."

"Oh, near the south end of town."

"Ah, we are evasive. I guess it will take some long drives home before I find out the truth about the mystery lady."

Without thinking, the words just jumped out of my mouth. "No, it won't."

I left it at that. He looked at me in a peculiar way, but he didn't ask any more questions. As he turned down my street, he looked over at me in an odd way again. I felt so embarrassed because there was a drug transaction going on right in front of my building and the guys even came over to the car to see if he wanted anything. He just shook his head and waved them on.

I looked at him and said, "I'm sorry."

"What do you have to be sorry for? We all have to start out somewhere."

"Yeah, as soon as I get a couple of checks, I plan on moving."

"That's great, and we'll make sure that you stay long enough to keep it."

"Thanks for the ride."

Kyle got out of the car to open the door for me. I thought he was so chivalrous. No one had ever gotten out of the car to open the door for me before. Too bad, he was married. As I was walking away, he called out, "Nikki."

I turned around.

"See you tomorrow, right?"

"Yes, Kyle, I'll be there with bells on."

He threw up his hand, got back in his car and drove away.

The next day, I decided to go in to work early. When I got there, Kyle and Joel were already in the office, and they were not having a good day to start with. I went to make coffee and as I passed Joel's office, I could hear loud talking, not yelling but the voices were loud. Kyle was saying something about how he hired him when no one else would and that he expected more respect from him. Joel seemed not to care because he was just as vociferous when he said he had been Kyle's patsy long enough. I quickly hurried back down the hall just as quietly as I could. When I looked up, Robert was standing at the end of the hall, looking at me.

"Are you all right?" he asked.

"Yes, but Kyle and Joel are not, and I don't want to disturb them."

He laughed, "You better get used to that around here."

I saw Kyle when he came out of Joel's office. I could tell that something was wrong. He looked down the hall at me, then went into his office and slammed the door. Joel followed suit shortly thereafter and slammed his own door shut. I decided to go ahead and make the coffee. After it had brewed, I went to Kyle's office and knocked on the door.

"Come in," he said somewhat harshly.

"I brought you a cup of coffee."

"I'm sorry. I thought you were someone else. You're a godsend, thank you."

I put the steaming cup on his desk, and he handed me his mug.

"Would you be a dear and put mine in this?"

"Sure."

I took his cup, which I had to wash, and headed down the hall. On the way, I passed Robert's office and peeked in.

"I made coffee. Would you like for me to bring you a cup, or if you have your own cup, I can pour it for you?"

"No, thanks, Nikki, I don't drink the stuff."

"Okay, so what do you drink?"

"Please don't bother yourself with it. It's no big deal."

"You sure?"

"Yes, I'm sure."

I went down to the ladies' room to wash Kyle's cup, then took it back to his office.

"You're too good to us; if you keep this up, we'll have to keep you on forever."

"That would be wonderful. Just call the agency and tell them that."

He smiled, then I had to run down the hall because the telephone started ringing. I forgot I had taken it off the message machine. It was a call for Joel, but as I was attempting to transfer it, he came down the hall.

"I'll be out of the office for a while."

"You have a call on line one. What do you want me to do with it?"

He looked at me in the oddest way, and I didn't want to ask again.

"I'll take care of it," I said.

He mumbled something as he walked towards the elevator. As the elevator door opened, he stepped in and sarcastically said, "That *is* your job, isn't it?"

The doors closed. I got so mad. When I picked up the call, I could hardly speak. Then Karan came in. I told her I needed to speak with her.

"Let me just put my things down first."

When she came back, I told her what transpired between Joel and me.

"Honey, I really don't know what to tell you, except if it gets worse, go to Kyle with it. But don't expect anything to really happen. For some reason, Kyle will let a person go before he will get into it with Joel."

I told her that I had overheard them arguing this morning.

"Yeah, but I'm sure it was nothing serious. When it is serious around here, you will surely know it without a doubt."

"Wow, does it get *really* bad sometimes?"

She nodded her head.

My day had started in a peculiar mood, and I wasn't sure which way it would end. It seemed all day long, if the telephone wasn't ringing with some rude client, then it was a rude client coming into the office. Everyone had a short temper today.

Then I finally got the chance to meet with Ms. Buffy, and talk about *rude*, she was the queen mother. She sashayed into the office, wearing little to nothing and acting as if she owned the place. She was short and most of her height was her legs. She had long hair, or longed hair, as I say, for weaves, but I really could not tell right off. She was very tiny and looked like she could have been a model had she been taller. Buffy was very beautiful—until she opened her mouth. Her voice made my skin crawl. It was like a loud whine, and she talked through her nose. I couldn't believe that sound came out of her little body. She sounded like she was sick in bed.

"Is George in?" she asked, walking over to my desk.

"I can check and see. Who might I say is calling?"

She looked at me, rolled her eyes, and under her breath, I heard her say, "I *hate* new people."

I believe she thought I should automatically know who she was. I called George's office, but he didn't answer the telephone.

"He's not at his desk. Is there anything else I can do for you?"

"Well, *where is* he?"

"I'm not sure. I only know that he is not at his desk."

She looked at me as if she could kill me, and then she told me to tell him that his fiancée, Buffy, had come by.

"Would that be *Butty*?"

That *really* made her mad. She retorted, "No, *Buffy*!"

As if on cue, she turned on her 5" heals and stormed back to the elevator. I let out a little chuckle and went back to work. When George came in, he was with someone, a client, I guessed. He swung by my desk to ask if he had any calls. I told him that he hadn't, but that a Ms. Buffy came by. The look of a frightened little boy came over his face, and he turned and hurried down to his office, I guess to call her. I had never seen such a look on a grown man before. She terrified him. I could see that right away.

The rest of the day was quiet. We had little or no excitement like what we had experienced most of the morning, and so the day seemed to drag on. At 5:00, we shut down, and I got my things to go. I tried to get on the elevator before any of the associates got on, especially Joel, but I wasn't so lucky. Tom wobbled down the hall with Joel, who seemed to be in an okay mood, and that was just fine with me. Once we were in the elevator, we said nothing. When we got off, we still said nothing. I went to my bus stop, hoping that Kyle was not leaving anytime soon. When I got there, it was raining. I stood as close to the door as I possibly could without missing my bus or getting wet. I didn't see Robert when he drove up. It was too messy to see well, but he blew his horn and rolled down the window.

"Can I give you a lift?"

I told him that I was all right, but he responded, "Oh, come on, I don't bite."

I immediately knew that I worked with some very nice people—at least most of them.

"Thank you." I really was glad for the ride. I was just reluctant to be asking for favors so soon. When I got into the car, I noticed a familiar scent, but I couldn't put my finger on it right then. It smelled heavenly.

"Where do you live?" he asked.

I told him. He didn't flinch or make a face. He just said, "Okay." As he drove, he said, "You didn't bring an umbrella, did you?"

"No. How did you know that?"

"Well, no one expected rain today, not even the weatherman."

"That's true."

He didn't say much after that until we got in front of my building, then he said, "Hold on."

Of course, rain does nothing for the "working boys" of the neighborhood, but at least they did not try to approach him. Robert opened the door and went to his trunk. Then he came around to my side of the car and opened the door, holding an umbrella. I thought he was so wonderful. With a smile, he walked me all the way up to the entryway of my building.

"Thank you," I said gratefully.

He waved good-bye as he walked back to his car. I thought, *Now there is a man that would never take advantage of a girl.*

Chapter 2

A couple of weeks went by and Kyle had not asked me to lunch again. He had not even offered to take me home. I wondered if it had anything to do with Robert taking me home, but I did not want to make any assumptions. It could have been because of the case they got a while back. They had all been working overtime on it. One day while I was going through the mail, Ms. Buffy comes up, wearing tight black leather and demanded to see George, but this time she called him Mr. Thimberton.

"One moment, please."

She stood in front of me tapping her shoes until I made the call. George was in with a client and could not see her now. I conveyed the message to her. She was furious. She walked around in a circle, demanding, "How *dare* he?"

I just kept on sorting my mail. When she started down the hall, I stopped her.

"Mr. Thimberton is in a meeting and can not be disturbed at the moment."

She sat down in a huff. "I'll wait!"

I started to call him and tell him what was happening, but decided against it. I went to deliver the mail, first to Robert. He was sitting at his desk, looking out of the window.

"A penny for your thoughts," I said standing in his doorway.

As he smiled, he said, "Well, these thoughts run about $100 an hour."

"Well, how about just a second of your time."

11

"Sure."

I entered his office. I wanted to thank him for taking me home the other week, but I had not seen much of him because the attorneys were all so busy.

"It was no big deal. I'm sure that any of the other associates would have done the same thing if they had seen you."

"Well, maybe everyone but Joel."

He looked up at me and chuckled. "Don't get Joel wrong. He's just in a bad situation and is not happy, so he does not want anyone else to be happy."

I wanted to know more but realized that it was not my place to ask.

"Well, I brought you something."

"What is it?"

"Usually when I meet someone who doesn't like coffee, I find that they are hot chocolate fans."

"Really?"

"I've found this really nice chocolate place that makes hot chocolate from scratch with real bits of chocolate, and I've bought you some."

"You shouldn't have done that."

"It was the least I could do. You saved me from the rain."

I gave him his mail and the package that I had wrapped for him. He had the biggest grin on his face, as if he was not used to anyone giving him anything, I could tell. He accepted it graciously. As I closed the door, I said, "Bye," checking to see if he was opening the bag.

I moved on to the next office and knocked on Tom's door.

"Come in."

I did, but when I walked through the door, he jumped. I don't think he was expecting anyone.

"I just brought the morning mail."

He almost stuttered when he said, "Leave it on the desk and thank you."

"Tom, is there anything I can get for you?"

"No, you are really helpful."

"Okay."

As I turned to walk out the door, he said, "You are the nicest receptionist we have ever had. I hope you stay."

I turned to him with a smile. "Thank you, Tom, and if it was up to me, I would stay forever."

He smiled at me as I left his office. I was on my way back down the hall when I noticed Ms. Buffy was not sitting in the front anymore. I figured she was upset and left, but when I went to give George his mail, she was sitting there in his office.

"Oh, I have your mail."

He gave me a disdainful look as I laid the mail on his desk. I continued my route by going to Joel's office next, but on the way to his office, I wondered what that "look" was about. I knocked on Joel's door and heard him respond dryly, "Come in."

"I have your mail."

He looked at me as if to say, "So what?" as I put it on his desk.

"I have a bin for that."

"I'm sorry, I wasn't aware of one."

"If you would take the time to look, you would have seen it has been there for a week."

I picked up the mail and put it in the bin marked "mail." Then I walked out of the door. I wanted to slam the door, but thought if I wanted to keep my job, that would not be the professional thing to do. After that, I went over to Kyle's office. His door was ajar, but I still knocked. He motioned me in because he was on the phone. I showed him the mail, he pointed to the desk and I placed the mail in his in-box, then prepared to leave the office. Kyle waved his hand for me to have a seat. Suddenly I got nervous. *Why would he want me to have seat?* As I sat down, I tried to smile. He continued his phone conversation while making hand jokes about the person on the other end. Apparently, that person just kept talking, even when Kyle said, "Yeah, well, I'll have to get back with you on that."

He had said that about four times while I was sitting there. Then he finally said, "I'll have to call you back on that." Then he hung up the phone.

"Some people! So, Nikki, how are you? Do you like our little family now?"

"Everyone is so wonderful to me."

"Well, that's what I'm talking about."

My heart stopped. I thought he was going to fire me. I tried to think of what I might have done, but then, it could have been Joel. He didn't like me for some reason.

"Well, sir, if there is something I'm not doing right, I'll work harder on it."

Kyle laughed. "Oh, no, you aren't doing anything wrong. On the contrary, everyone here thinks that you're doing a wonderful job, and we want you to stay."

I had a grin on my face as wide as the Grand Canyon.

"Really?"

He said, "Yes, really. I have already called the agency and asked what we needed to do to get you to stay. They said that basically, it was a matter of paying a fee to get out of the contract and then the decision would be yours."

"I'd love to stay, sir."

He said, "Well, then, welcome to the company. If you go and talk with Karan, I have already given her the information for your salary and benefits."

"Thank you, Kyle, thank you very much."

"No, you earned it. I would not offer you the job if you had not proven yourself to me." He held out his hand and as I shook it, he said, "Welcome to the firm."

Inside, I felt all giggly. I floated out the door, down to Karan's office. When I knocked on the door, she said, "Come in."

"Kyle just told me the news."

She looked at me and said, "What news?"

The smile evaporated from my face. "He wants me here permanently."

"Oh, really? He didn't say anything to me."

"Oh, I thought he had."

"No. I'll go and talk with him later about it."

"Okay."

I gave her the mail and walked out of the office. Perplexed, I went back to my desk and started answering the phones. A little while later, Karan came to my desk and asked if she could talk with me in the bathroom.

"Sure."

She had a serious look on her face, so I knew it wasn't gossip. When I got there, she just said that she had not been able to talk with Kyle yet but that she would get with him as soon as possible. She told me that I had something on my face and that maybe I should wash it off before going back to my desk. I looked but did not see anything. I decided to rinse my face anyway. As she walked out the door, she told me to meet her in the break room first. When I got there, Kyle, George, Robert, and Tom were in there with a big cookie that said, "Welcome aboard, Nikki!" I turned and hugged her, and she started laughing.

"I had you going, didn't I?"

"Yeah, you sure did."

We stayed in there for about 15 to 20 minutes with everyone congratulating me and me cutting the cookie. Everyone seemed genuinely happy and, of course, I didn't expect Joel to be happy, which was probably why he wasn't there. After that joyous time, I went back to answering the phone lines. Karan came by to tell me that she would have to get with me later this week to fill out some paperwork, discuss my salary and inform me about the benefits package. I was so excited I could have gotten a million bad calls that day and it would have been okay, but as it turned out, I only got one.

George called me to his office after everything had settled down. He asked me to close the door, which I did. As I sat down, he said, "I want to congratulate you again and welcome you into our family."

"Thank you," I said smiling.

"That is what we are, a family."

I just sat there and paid attention.

"I don't want to tell you how to run the front office because I think that on a regular basis, you are doing a damned good job. We haven't had any complaints about your attitude, and you appear to be busy, even when things are going slow. You always dress professionally, and you have a very cheerful personality that radiates throughout the office."

"Thank you."

He continued, "Earlier today, I was in a meeting with a client, and somehow, one of my guests got past you and interrupted a meeting I was having. Luckily, I was just finishing it when she burst into the office, but it could have been a terrible situation for everyone."

I nodded my head as if to let him know I understood.

"In the future, will you please make sure you let the associates know if there appears to be a problem with any of the guests or clients that may enter the lobby area? We have put you in control of it, and it is in your domain to keep everything under control."

"I'm very sorry it happened, and I'll try to do better."

"I did not take this up with anyone else because it's a small matter. I'm not trying to scold you. Just please be more careful next time. Thanks. I'm finished."

I left the office and felt bad because I hadn't been able to stop her. Here I was, the receptionist, and I could not control the reception area. When lunchtime came, I joined Karan. We went to a little salad place downstairs, and I told her what happened.

"Well, we all make mistakes. You just need to make sure that the lobby is covered most of the time."

"I had to deliver the mail."

"It happens, so don't worry about it, because it could have been worse, but it wasn't."

I still felt bad and didn't want to pry, but I had to ask, "So what's going on with Ms. Buffy and George?"

"Well, you know I don't like to gossip, but it appears that he took the ring back."

I asked, "Why?"

She said, "I'm not sure, I just know that he has."

I asked her how she got her information. Looking up from her meal with a sly little grin, she said, "Well, I was the first receptionist they had, and I know a lot of the people that they know now. So I get little tidbits from their friends' secretaries and all sorts of people here in the building."

"Wow."

"Yeah, you'll learn. It's all about who you know."

By evening, all was well, and George was back to his kidding self again. I got ready to go to the elevators, and there was Robert, holding the elevator door. We rode down together; and he asked me if I needed a lift home.

"I don't think it's raining today."

"Me either, I just thought that you might want to ride with me instead of taking the bus."

"Sure, thanks."

We went on down to the garage. When I got into the car, it had that familiar scent again.

"I don't mean to pry, but the scent in your car is so familiar. What is it?"

"It should be, that is, if you pay any attention to me at all. It's the only scent that I wear, and I got a bottle for my car so that I keep myself surrounded by things that I like."

"Okay, and you still have not answered my question."

He smiled and said in a shy way as if I had hurt his feelings, "It's Fahrenheit."

"That's nice. I've never heard of it, but it smells so wonderful."

"Thanks, I like it."

"And you are right; it *is* the scent for you." I said this without looking over at him but from the corner of my eye, I saw when he looked over at me. I had hoped he had gotten the hint. Yes, I *had* been paying attention. Who wouldn't be? He was an Adonis. I knew that Karan had pretty much said that he was off-limits, but so was I, and if he didn't jump at that little flirtation, I knew I was safe.

Chapter 3

By now, I had been a permanent employee of The Peoples Law Firm for one month. Life was good, and I felt that if things kept going this way, I would be able to move out of my apartment and maybe buy a car. Most of the guys were pretty nice about giving me a ride home, especially when it rained, but mostly I had been riding with Robert when he wasn't working late or didn't have anything to do. Karan came to my desk to see if anyone had come or called her after lunch.

"No, but I'll let you know if they do."

She said, "Oh, by the way, you sure are getting cozy with Robert."

"What do you mean?"

"Well, I've noticed you two leaving at the same time, and when I get outside, I don't see you standing at the bus stop anymore."

"I admit he has taken me home on a couple of occasions, but it's nothing special."

"Well, just don't get too used to it; you know we have to remember our places."

I lowered my eyes and said, "Yeah."

I didn't want to talk with her anymore today. I was mad. What did she mean by "our places"? Was she trying to say that I couldn't date someone like Robert? I went through the day not saying anything to anyone. Kyle had seen me on several occasions today and finally, he asked me if I wanted to have lunch with him.

"Sure," I said, even though that might not be my place.

On the drive to lunch, Kyle said, "I don't mean to be nosy, but is there something wrong?"

"No, why would you say that?"

"Well, you're usually a very happy person, and it radiates from you, but today, your light is a little dim."

"Well, someone said something that I didn't think was nice."

"Is it something I should be concerned about? It wasn't Joel, was it?"

Turning to him, I said, "No."

"Well, if it isn't any of my business, then I won't ask again."

"Thank you."

I turned back towards the window. We got to the restaurant and had a good lunch. Kyle cheered me up and made me laugh. On the way back to the office, I said, "Thank you."

"No problem. It was my pleasure. Now, do you want to tell me what's wrong?"

"No, not really. It's just someone commented on Robert taking me home sometimes and said that I should remember *my place.*"

"Oh, that wasn't nice."

"Yeah, I know."

"What do you think about it?"

"There's nothing to think about. Sometimes Robert sees me at the bus stop, and he's nice enough to take me home. Heck, you've done it too."

He smiled and said, "Yes, I have. I wouldn't worry about it if I were you. They are probably just jealous that he isn't offering them a ride home."

I told him that I would get over it soon.

"Good, you're too pretty to be walking around with a sour face."

That cheered me up more. It had been a long time since anyone implied that I was pretty. We got back to the office, and I started catching up on my work. People came and went all afternoon. I got ready to leave for the evening, and there was Robert already at the elevator. I didn't remember seeing him go by my desk. I started walking towards the elevator and tried to act as if I had left something at my desk. I turned away, and he said, "Hey, I'll hold the elevator for you. Hurry up."

20 | *Felicia Truttier*

In my head, I said *damn*. I turned around to go back into the office. Robert stayed there holding it for me. I ran inside and came back.

"Thank you."

"No problem."

We didn't say anything for a couple of floors. Then he said pleasantly, "Are you riding with me today?"

"Oh, you don't have to do that. I can take the bus."

"Yes, I know, but it's really no trouble, and it is on my way."

"Well, I really need to stop at the market before going home."

"Great, I'll take you."

"No, really, it's okay."

Then he said, "You're not going to take groceries home on the bus, are you? I insist."

"Okay," I said with resignation.

Damn! I'm trapped.

As we were getting into the car, I saw Karan pass us. She even blew her horn to let me know that she had seen us. I closed my eyes.

Robert said, "Are you okay?"

"Oh, yeah, sure."

He suggested a market by his home, which really wasn't that far from my place.

"How could you live this close to me and the areas be so different?"

He laughed and said, "You know, I never thought of it."

The marketplace over by his home was so nice and clean. They even had a place were you could eat before you shopped. They carried a lot of stuff the stores by me didn't have, and I went ahead and bought more than I normally do. We had a ball in the grocery store. Robert asked me all kinds of questions about what I ate and then sometimes he would say "yuck" to something that I would pick up. It was funny. He seemed so limited in what he would eat. I told him that he just needed a good home cooked meal. Then he asked if that was an invitation. I closed my mouth and went to the other aisle. He came behind me and didn't say anything.

We didn't really talk again until we got to the car. While driving me home, Robert said, "Are you that ashamed of where you live?"

I just said the first thing I was thinking. "That I'm a receptionist, and you're a lawyer, and we have our places."

"Oh, I'm sorry. I didn't mean to offend you."

He took me to the front of my building. I didn't realize how much stuff I had gotten, but my pride would not let that stand in the way. I somehow grabbed everything and barely able to walk, I made it to my building. I didn't even turn around to see if he was still there.

Chapter 4

I got to work late the next morning, and everything was going crazy. Karan was sitting at my desk answering the phones. She looked like all hell had broken loose. Even though I was only 15 minutes late, it seemed like everyone and their mother had called and obviously, she had forgotten how to run the front desk. There were little sticky notes everywhere. Karan looked as if she had been running her hands through her hair all morning. I ran over to the desk and said, "I'm sorry I overslept."

She smiled, "Oh, that's okay, it's just I haven't done this in a while."

I got the next call and transferred him accordingly.

"Thanks, girl."

"No problem, thank you."

"Did you have a nice time?"

"Doing what?"

"Well, I saw you leave with Robert, and I had a question, so I called you when I got home."

I looked at her and said, "No, we didn't go out. I had to run to the grocery store, and he was kind enough to take me."

"Yes, he is that sweet, isn't he?"

I sighed and said, "What was the question?"

"What question?"

"The one you needed an answer to last night."

She said, "Oh, well, I figured it out myself."

With that, she turned and walked towards the break room. I mumbled to myself, "I hope this isn't going to be blown out of proportion," and to my surprise, Robert came in at that exact moment.

"What doesn't get blown out of proportion?"

I looked up surprised, wondering how much he had heard.

"Oh, nothing. How are you this morning?"

"Fine, and I hope that things are better with you today."

"Not so far."

He stopped on his way to his office and said, "Nikki, am I bothering you?"

I shook my head in response. "Why would you say that?"

"It just seems like lately you don't want to be bothered, and I would not like to be the one to get on your nerves."

I thought now I was about to alienate one of my bosses. I followed him into his office.

"Well, some people have been noticing you taking me home, and I don't think it looks good."

He said, "For whom? Do you have a boyfriend that is getting upset?"

"No, but I don't like gossip getting started around the office."

"Oh, I see. Well, I don't want to cramp your style. I won't offer to give you any more rides home."

"That's not the reason."

"Well, what do you expect me to think?"

I turned and looked at the door. "Maybe it isn't a good idea that you take me home anymore."

"That's fine with me if that's the way you want it."

I turned and walked out of the door. I felt terrible, and now I was back on the bus. *What else could possibly happen now? What was I was thinking? What else?* Shortly after that, I thought things were going to get better. They didn't. In walked Ms. Buffy. She was dressed in a short little leather outfit and some long thigh boots. I wondered what planet was she from.

I said, "Yes," as pleasantly as I could. "How may I help you?"

"H E L L O. I'm here to see George."

I told her she would have to take a seat until I could reach him. Then I paged his office, but he wasn't in it.

"Excuse me, miss."

She stood up, walked to my desk, and said with attitude, "The name is *Buffy*, sweetie."

I said back with more attitude, "Well, Buffy, it appears that Mr. Thimberton is out of the office."

"And do you know when he might return?"

"No, it's early morning, and no one has informed me of anything yet."

"In that case, I'll wait."

I shook my head and let my eyes roll up. She sat there as quietly and politely as she could, sometimes standing and asking when the phone rang if that was him. I would say no, and then she would sit back down. He finally did call, and I was trying to be evasive.

"Hello, sir, how may I help you?"

He said, "Nikki, this is George. Have I had any calls?"

"No, sir."

"Well, I'll be in shortly. I'm on my way."

"That's wonderful, sir, but we seemed to have a situation going on right now."

"Are you all right?"

"Yes, sir, but we have a situation going on right now, *in the office*."

I could see that Ms. Buffy was looking up at me, trying to see whom I was talking to.

"That you don't need to come into the place right now."

He still didn't catch on. Finally, he said, "Are you trying to tell me something?"

"Yes, sir!"

"Someone is in the office?"

"Yes, sir!"

"Is it Buffy?"

"Yes, sir."

He said, "Shit!"

"Is there anything you need for me to do?"

"Yeah, just let me know when she leaves. I'm not coming in right now. I'll call back later."

"Will do. As soon as he gets in, I'll let you know."

He said, "Thanks, Nikki, and I'm sorry about the curse word."

"No problem, I completely understand."

Ms. Buffy sat there picking at her nails, then at her teeth. Periodically she would come and ask if he had called or if I was sure that he was coming in.

"No to both questions."

After a couple of hours, I went to take the mail around. When I got to Joel's office, he said, "I hope that you know you aren't allowed to have overnight guests in the office."

I dropped his mail off and left the room. When I got to Kyle's office, he asked me if I knew where George was and why Buffy was still out in the lobby.

"He is apparently trying to avoid her, and she will not move," I told him.

"Well, this isn't the first time they have gone through one of their break-up routines, but she always gets him back."

"Really?"

"Yeah, really. The last time she waited out there for about 4 hours while he was taking some depositions, then the two of them were in his office for quite some time after that. I suspected making up."

"And that didn't bother you?"

"Why? I couldn't prove anything. I just suspected it, and besides, no one was hurt by it.

"I need for you to remind me to have a talk with him about that. I don't mind her coming up here, but this is a business, and they need to handle their business at home."

He smiled in a sneaky way, I guess to imply something to me. He continued, "But Nikki, I understand that sometimes you have To Do THE THING when you have TO DO THE THING."

I caught on to that hint and started my way quickly out of the office. When I got to Tom's office, he was on the phone, so I just left the mail on his desk. He smiled as he watched me put the mail down and leave. I waved bye to him before leaving his office, and I believe he turned pale.

When I got to Robert's office, he just said hello. No, smile no nothing, just a dry hello. I figured I deserved that. I left his mail on his desk. No reply was necessary. I knew he didn't want one anyway. I got to George's office, but his door was closed so I took his mail back with me. When I got to Karan's office, she said, "Come in and close the door."

I came in.

"Is that Buffy girl still out there?"

"Yes," I said.

"She's a pest."

"I've heard how persistent she can bet."

"What are you doing for lunch?"

I told her if Buffy didn't leave, I'd be eating at my desk, because I promised George I would keep a watch.

She said, "Girl, don't get entangled in that mess. They go through this about every 6 months or so. She'll get mad and throw the engagement ring at him. Then she gets over it and will come back, saying that she was sorry for being a bad girl, and he always takes her back. The other part is with you playing on his side right now, it's only going to make it bad for you when they get back together. Believe me, Buffy will not forget that you betrayed her."

"Why is that?"

"Because Buffy will remember that you were against her, and she is a true bitch. She will try to make your life a living hell, and when they are together, he is her devoted slave."

"Well, what should I do?"

She said, "Don't do too much on either hand. The next time she comes in, just call him and tell him she's there, but don't try to make it seem like you're trying to keep anything from her."

"Why should I be sucking up to her? She doesn't sign my check."

"I know, but her baby pays for some of it."

"Yeah, point well taken."

I started walking out the door. I thought she would say something about Robert, but she didn't, so I went on to my desk. Buffy just sat there, and there she sat for the rest of the day. I thought he must really be mad this time. He had called one more time to say that he wasn't going to come in today and that if there were any important calls, to transfer them to his cell phone. I replied by saying that I would and asked if I should relay the message to the guest waiting in the lobby. He said sure, he really didn't care.

After I hung up the phone, I said, "Excuse me, miss."

She gave me a look that could kill.

Again, I said, "Excuse me. Buffy, I just received a call from Mr. Thimberton, and he said that he would not be in for the rest of the day."

"So he just called? Did you tell him that I was here—waiting all day?"

"Yes, ma'am."

She stood up obviously mad at the world, but mostly mad at George, turned, and stomped towards the elevator door. I was relieved. I hadn't eaten all day, and my stomach was growling. As I started packing things up, Kyle walked out of his office and said, "Nikki, are you leaving?"

"Yeah, unless you want to pay me some overtime."

He laughed, and so did I.

"Would you like a ride home instead? I don't have any plans tonight."

I looked down the hall towards Robert's office and said, "Sure."

As far as I knew, Robert had not left, but I was sure he would not ask—not after the things I said today. I got my things together, and we headed towards the elevator. Tom and Robert both met us there. I said to myself, *Oh, yeah, this looks right.*

While on the elevator, Kyle started talking like no one else was there with us. He said, "You didn't take a lunch break today, did you?"

"No, I was on third watch with Ms. Buffy."

"Well, I didn't get to eat what I really wanted myself. Do you want to go and catch a bite?"

My stomach growled a yes, but I looked at the back of Robert's head and said, "No, thanks."

But he persisted, "Well, we could just stop someplace on the way."

I wanted to sink through the floor. Was he *advertising* the fact that he was taking me home? Tom tried not to look interested, but you could tell he was all ears.

"I'll be all right until I get home."

"I insist, because you worked through your lunchtime, and I want to make it up to you."

I finally said yes just to shut him up. The elevator stopped at the garage, and everyone got off. Robert said, "Everybody have a good night."

We all wished him one, too. I could not believe what had just happened. I knew that he would be too mad at me, but what else could I do? When we got to Kyle's car, he was in the Mercedes this time. We sat in the car for a minute before he said, "Were you uncomfortable in the elevator just a few minutes ago?"

I lied. "Uncomfortable? About what? Oh no, I wasn't uncomfortable about anything."

I could tell he knew I was lying, but I had started it now and couldn't take it back.

"Good. I'm not just your boss, you know. I'm a friend, and if you need someone to confide in, I can be that person."

I looked down at my hands. "Thanks, but everything is okay."

We drove off. We went to a Mexican restaurant not too close to my house. I thought he said it would be on the way. The place was really nice, but it was kind of out of the way, like the kind of place a person would take his mistress or someone like that. I started getting nervous. *What if he really made a pass at me, how would I get home and more importantly, when I told him no, would he fire me?* All these things were running through my mind as I watched him watch me, so I blurted out, "You come here often?"

"No, I used to."

I couldn't tell if it was a lie or the truth. He could still be bringing someone here, or he might bring someone else here after I turn him down.

He said, "Things change, and so do people."

I said, "Yeah, they do."

"Now, what's your story? Why don't you have a boyfriend, or girlfriend, for that matter?"

He laughed at himself for that one. I knew that he often tried to be funny, but tonight, I didn't want it to seem like I wanted him coming onto me so I didn't laugh.

"Well, I don't have a boyfriend because I broke up with him over a year ago, and I don't have a girlfriend because girls can be a bitch to date." I laughed at that one.

"And basically, I haven't been looking for anyone. I've been taking this time to get to know who I am, and I'm finding out that I'm a pretty good person with or without a man."

He said, "Yeah, but there are some things women need a man for."

"Oh, really, like what?" I said.

"Well, like changing the light bulb," he replied.

"I can change the light bulb just fine."

He continued, "Well, what about ...?"

I looked at him waiting for him to say it.

"Well, what about on those cold winter nights when the heater goes out?"

My reply was, "I have an electric blanket, and it won't bother me if I have to go without a shower."

"You are going to make me say it, aren't you?"

"I don't know what you're talking about."

"Well, what about sex?"

"Oh, that. Well, there are all kinds of things that women do so they don't have to have sex with a man."

"Really? Tell me some."

"Well, we read."

Then I looked up at the expression on his face. He said, "Oh? And you read ...?"

"I've been reading since I was 4."

He chuckled at that one. "Okay, but it isn't the same as having sex with a man."

"Reading is fundamental and well as sex; sex can get you into a whole lot of trouble."

"Not if you have sex with the right person."

I knew that we were about to get into an uncomfortable area, so I started looking around the restaurant and commenting on how authentic it looked. I had eaten almost all of the tortilla chips and salsa and was hoping someone would interrupt us with our meal soon.

He said, "What else do women like you do to relieve the tensions of sex?"

"We do yoga, and we go to the movies a lot."

"You don't do anything with yourself to get fulfilled?"

"Well, I'm sure some women do, but I can't speak for every one of them."

"That's good. I'm only interested in talking to one of them."

I crunched down on my last chip. I had been trying to make it linger, but time seemed to be running out. I didn't really want to address that statement, so I jumped up and said, "I have to go to the ladies' room. I'll be right back."

"I'll be here waiting."

I went to the front of the restaurant to find out were the restroom was. I needed some time. I wanted some time to think. I didn't want to lose my job, but I was not going to sleep with this married man. I stayed in the bathroom a while, hoping that when I got back to the table, our food would be there and I would not have to talk about sex with him anymore. Eventually, I walked back to the table and luckily, our food was there.

Kyle said, "I started to send the National Guard out looking for you."

"I was just doing a woman's thing."

"Oh, yeah, I forgot. You girls spend a lot of time in the bathroom. You need to go and 'freshen up' and all of that."

I sighed and breathed deeply.

"Can we get back on our conversation?"

I suggested, "How about let's eat first since that's what we came here for."

"Well, if that's what you want."

"Yes, it is."

We ate in silence but every now and then, he would ask me a question or two and I would answer it as best as I could. After the meal, Kyle drove me home. When we got in front of my building, he asked if I needed him to walk me up.

"I'm all right."

"I'm worried about you walking around out here this time of night."

"You need to be more worried with you and this car out here this time of night."

He laughed but the look on his face was serious. I got out of the car and walked to my building. When I turned to wave at him, he was already gone. That made me laugh really hard.

Chapter 5

I arrived at work bright and early the next morning only to find that when I got to the downstairs elevator, I was surprised to find Ms. Buffy there waiting. We rode up the elevator together, and she didn't say a word. Once we stepped into the empty office, she began, "Do you think that George, or Mr. Thimberton, as you like to call him, will be coming in this morning?"

"I'm not aware if he is or isn't. As you can plainly see, I have just gotten to work and have not been able to check the office messages."

"OK, I'll wait over there," she said, pointing to the same love seat she had been occupying for the last 2 days, and then sat down. As everyone entered the office, the first thing they noticed was Buffy occupying the leather couch. They looked at me with a smirk on their faces, then each went to his office. I checked all the messages from last night and transferred them to the associate they belonged to. There was one message for me. It was George saying that Buffy had called and left a message on his answering machine saying that she would be up here first thing this morning and that he would definitely not be in until she left. My instructions were to tell her that he would not be in today and as soon as she left, to page him or call his cell phone. I did as I was instructed. She sat there for a moment contemplating the situation before she stormed out, saying that she would be back tomorrow and that he could not hide from her forever. I shook my head and said in a low voice so no one would hear me, "Damn, people are *so* weird."

I went to the break room to make the morning coffee. As I went taking everyone their cup, I passed by Joel's office and noticed that he was sitting there with the weirdest look on his face. He seemed to be in deep thought over something, but I wasn't sure what it was. I wondered what he was cooking up in his evil little mind. Kyle was on a conference call and waved thanks for the coffee. Tom was just Tom going through some paperwork and said, "Thanks."

As usual, I knocked on Karan's door, but she was engulfed in some deep conversation and just waved me away. I took the remainder cup for myself. I wanted to stop by Robert's office but felt maybe it wasn't a good time. So I sat at my desk, turned on the office music, and waited for the morning mail. Out of nowhere came this shout that sounded like Joel.

"Christ Almighty!"

I think we all heard it. I wanted to run down the hall and see if everything was okay, but it was just Joel, so I remained at my desk. He came running down the hall and loudly inquired,

"When did this mail come?"

"I don't know. What do you mean?"

"I've been looking for this piece of mail for a week. The client said they sent it over 2 weeks ago, and I *just now* find it in my basket."

"I put the mail there when it comes in every morning and every evening."

"This postmark on here says a week ago."

"It must have come a week ago then."

"What are you saying—that I did something with it for a whole week, and now I just want to blame you?"

"I don't know what you did with the mail, but if you just got it, then it only came yesterday."

I told him that when the mail comes in, I sort it, put it in order of the offices, and then I take it to the associate it belongs to.

He responded, "That sounds like a sound system, *if* that's what you do with it."

My mouth dropped open. I couldn't believe what I was hearing. He was accusing *me* of holding important mail.

"I do not appreciate you blaming me."

By this time, both of us had gotten a little loud, and Karan hurried out of her office.

"What's the matter?"

Illegal Love | 33

I tried to explain what Joel said happened, but he interrupted me and said, "She lost some very important mail of mine, and now she's trying to pass it off as coming in yesterday."

"I did no such thing," I shouted.

Karan said, "Joel, calm down."

He didn't.

"I don't have to do anything. You're just an office manager, and what you need to be doing is managing your office."

With that, he stormed down the hall to Kyle's office.

"What bug flew up his ass?"

Karan said, "Now is *not* the time for jokes, Nikki. You know that the documents and mail that come through here are date sensitive."

"Karan, I swear I did not lose a piece of mail and try to pass it off as yesterday's mail. I would have come to you and told you that I misplaced a piece of mail if I had done that."

"I know that you would have."

We stood there trying to figure out what happened, and then Kyle called us to his office. Joel was sitting down huffing and puffing like a steamship.

Karan said, "Kyle, she said she did *not* do it."

"I know."

Everyone looked at him.

He said, "It was accidentally put in my stack, and I forgot to give it to Joel."

I breathed a sigh of relief. He continued, "But the fact remains that it was put with the wrong mail."

I tried to figure out how I had done that or possibly when. "I'm sorry."

Joel said, "Yeah, what about the poor sucker who might lose his case the *next* time something like this happens."

Kyle said, "Joel, shut up."

If things had been different, I would have laughed at that—but they weren't. Kyle said, "We need to set up a better way so that this will not happen again. Maybe we should get a 'received stamp' so that Nikki can stamp the mail when she gets it."

Joel retorted, "She could *always* change the date to whatever she wanted it to say."

Again, Kyle said, "Joel, I told you to shut up." Then Kyle looked at me and said, "You won't do that, will you, Nikki?"

34 | *Felicia Truttier*

"No, I won't."

Kyle said, "Karan, you and Nikki go and figure out a better system for sorting the mail, and I'll try to calm Joel down."

We replied, "Okay."

As we turned to go out the door, Kyle said "Nikki, we all make mistakes. The best thing to do is to try and learn from this and make the next situation better."

"Yes, sir."

I had not called him sir in months but right now, I wanted to start calling him Mr. Simmons again. Karan and I went down the hall to her office, and I said, "I'm so sorry."

Over and over again ...

She said, "We all make mistakes."

"I don't know how I could have put the mail in the wrong office."

"Don't worry yourself over it. It happens. We just need to set up a system where it doesn't happen again, because next time, it could be too late."

I took a deep breath. "Okay, what do we do about the mail?"

"Right now, I don't know, but I should have some ideas by the end of the day."

I went back to my desk, trying to see if I remembered putting that particular piece of mail in Kyle's box. The more I tried to remember, the more I did not. By the time I got back to my desk, Tom came out of his office. He looked around to see if anyone was out there besides me, then he motioned me to come to his office. I went down the hall, looking back occasionally to see if anyone had come to my desk.

"Yes, Tom, can I help you?"

He said, "Well I, I, just want you, you to know that I don't think you did anything wrong."

"Thank you, Tom."

His stuttering had started, "You, you, you have to watch out for Joel. He isn't nice."

"I see. Well, I'll try to be more careful."

He said, "Good. That's all I wanted to say."

I walked out of the office and thought how sweet that was of him to speak with me that way. When I got back to my desk, the morning mail carrier was there. I thanked and then started sorting the mail. I had almost forgotten to call George back. I picked up the phone and called his cell number. He answered, and I told him that she was gone.

He said that he knew already and was on his way in.

Then I hung up the phone and sorted the mail as usual, but today, I wrote in the date, time, and initialed each piece. That done, the phone started ringing, so I answered it. A very deep and sexy voice on the other end said, "Good morning. May I speak with Kyle Simmons?"

"Yes, may I ask who's calling."

"Certainly. My name is Patrick Giddeons."

"Hold on, please."

I called Kyle's line. He sounded like he was displeased with something.

"There's a Patrick Giddeons on the line."

His mannerism changed abruptly, and he said, "Oh, please patch him through."

I did as I was told. Not too long after I had transferred the call to Kyle's office, he called me and told me to have all the associates meet him in the conference room immediately. Everyone but Joel was agreeable.

He said, "What does he want?"

"I wouldn't possibly know that. I'm only the receptionist," I replied, then I hung up the phone.

They were in there for a little while before George arrived. He walked through the door, and I said, "I think that you're missing a very important meeting."

"Really?" he replied.

"Yes, some guy name Patrick Giddeons called, and Kyle called a meeting with everyone in the conference room."

George said. "Okay," then he quickly ran down the hall. I could hear him apologizing by the time he hit the door.

When the door closed, Karan came out of her office. She was over at my desk in a hot second and asked, "What's going on?"

"Kyle called a meeting after he spoke with a Patrick Giddeons."

She said, "All hell is about to break loose."

"What's going on?"

"He gets into all kinds of trouble with the law. I'm surprised that he is still a client after all the stuff the associates have had to deal with regarding him."

"Do you know what the problem is now?"

Karan answered, "No, but I think it has something to with one of his babies' mamas."

"Are there many of them?"

She said, "As many states as he plays in probably."

"Well, his voice sounds wonderful."

She laughed and said, "Wait until you see him."

I told her that I didn't watch sports, and I wasn't sure who he was, but she said, "You'll find out."

I left the office wondering what that meant. Sometime during the day, the guys all came out of the conference room. Kyle told me that they would be ordering lunch in and that if I would be so kind as to go down to the cafeteria on the second floor and pick up their orders, they'd appreciate it. I wanted to say that I was the receptionist, not a girl Friday, but instead I answered, "Okay."

I also asked Karan if she wanted something from downstairs, and she said, "I'll go with you to pick it up."

"Cool."

She could be really nice sometimes when she wanted to. We got onto the elevator, and she pushed the sixth floor.

"Where are we going? That isn't the floor for the cafeteria."

She said, "I know, I just have to stop and talk with someone. You'll get to meet some of my friends."

We got off the elevator and went to room 620. Sitting in front of a huge desk was a woman with a headset on. Karan asked, "Hey, girl, how are things?"

"Nothing much here. How about you?"

Karan said, "This is Nikki, the new receptionist."

"Hello, Nikki."

Karan said, "Nikki, this is Niyokia. She's the person who knows what's going on in the whole building, so if there's something you want to know, call her. She'll know it."

Niyokia said, "Girl, don't listen to her. I only get a little information every now and again."

Then she continued, "So *you're* the one all the talk is about."

Karan gave her a look as if to say shut up, but it was too late. I had already heard it.

"What talk?"

She smiled. "Oh, nothing bad. It's just most of the girls in this building would die to be in your and Karan's shoes, working with all those muscles upstairs. Then you—an unknown—get to spend so much time with that Robert. Girl, don't he just make your knees go weak?"

On the defensive I said, "I haven't been spending any time with him. He has taken me home once or twice, that's all."

"Well, it's more than he has ever done for me."

She and Karan started laughing, then Karan said, "Hell, me, too."

Karan said, "And I have been working with him the longest!"

I was embarrassed, and I hadn't done anything; yet, they made me feel dirty somehow. I wanted to leave, but Karan had not gotten her latest gossip for the day, so instead of leaving, I barely listened as Niyokia went on about some guy on the 10th floor who was caught in the janitor's closet with his secretary.

Karan said, "Oh, he should have gotten a hotel room."

"Girl, he doesn't have any money. He's already started filing for bankruptcy."

"Really? When did this happen?"

I broke in. "I don't want to interrupt, but we do have to get the guys their lunch."

Niyokia looked at me with a wicked grin and said, "So? You're just dedicated."

Karan said, "Wait until she becomes their regular errand girl."

Niyokia laughed. "Yeah, ain't it the truth?"

When we got back on the elevator, I asked Karan if she had been telling people that Robert was giving me rides home. She looked at me with a straight face and said, "No, one day one of the girls saw you getting into the car with him and they called me to find out who you were. I just told them that you were the new receptionist. I told them it was innocent, but you know how a rumor mill is. I brought you down to meet Niyokia so she could talk with you herself and get it all cleared up with everyone else."

I believed her for some reason, and we talked as we went down to fetch lunch. We had so many bags that I was glad that she had come with me. I don't think I would have been able to get everything if she hadn't come.

When we got back to the office, all the attorneys were still in the conference room. We took their lunches in the room and laid everything out for them. While in there, I tried not to listen, but I did hear a little bit of what was going on. I heard Kyle say that they had to make sure his alibi was tight. Patrick had said that he was over at one of his girlfriends' house when the hit and run occurred and that Patrick had loaned his car to his brother, who, in turn, had loaned it to a so far undisclosed friend.

At that point, I turned to walk out of the room. It was then that I noticed that Karan had already left. When I got out in the lobby area, she came to my desk to inquire about what I had heard. I told her that Patrick was involved in a hit and run and he was tying to get out of it.

She said, "Girl, never let Kyle hear you say that you think one of his clients is guilty. He would probably fire you on the spot. Everyone is entitled to legal representation, and everyone is innocent until proven guilty, and then that depends on if they lose in the appeal process."

"Thanks for the information."

"But his ass *is* probably guilty. He always has the same excuse—he was with some girl when the bad deed was done, and it's never his fault. Of course, it isn't always the same girl, but it is the same excuse every time."

"Well, doesn't that mean that he didn't do it?"

"Hmm, according to the law, you're right, because he always gets off, but if your name is *always* coming up in stuff, then you're probably doing some of it. He can't be that stupid all the time. We'll see him at least twice a year for something or another. Sometimes I think he just likes to spend money because of what they charge him, but if it were me, I'd stay out of trouble."

She left me with a lot to think about for the rest of the day. Maybe that man was innocent of everything he was accused of, but stuff just kept happening to him. I thought about things that had happened to me in the past, things that I didn't think were really my fault, but if someone were looking from the outside, they would surely think that I was guilty or stupid. I just wanted to be fair, because I knew what it was like not to be treated fairly. By the end of the day, I was resolved to the fact that Mr. Giddeons was probably guilty of some of the stuff he did, but maybe not all. Then I got ready for my ride home. I was not prepared because I knew I would have to take the bus today since the guys were still in a meeting.

For the rest of the week, all the associates were wrapped up in this case. They took their lunches in the conference room and no one was available for anything. On occasions, they would break and come to check their messages. I was kind of lonely from not seeing them come in and out all day. I fixed coffee every morning as usual and took it in to them. Kyle was usually absorbed in something or other so he really didn't raise his hand for coffee, Robert would sometimes look up and smile, and then there was Tom, who always waved or smiled at me.

When I started out of the office, Kyle said, "Oh, Nikki."

"Sir?"

He waved it off then he said, "We're expecting Patrick Giddeons to come into the office today and as soon as he does, will you call me in the conference room or wherever I might be at the time?"

"Sure, Kyle."

He smiled, and I walked out of the room. As I walked down the hall I thought to myself he would come on a day that I thought I looked like crap. I went down to the ladies' room to see what a trifling mess I was in. It wasn't too bad, but I didn't have on any makeup—, which I only wore on special occasions anyway—but I would have liked to have some on today. Then I went down to Karan's office. She was on the phone as usual—probably gossiping. I told her that Patrick Giddeons was coming in today.

She said, "Oh, okay, just let the fellas know when he gets here."

"Okay."

As I left her office, I thought she would be more surprised or something. I don't know, but her lack of enthusiasm was not what I expected. Maybe she didn't like him; maybe he didn't like her. I went to my desk and anticipated the wait. Calls came and people came, but no Patrick Giddeons came. I just knew I would go to lunch and miss him, so I rushed downstairs to get a quick sandwich and promptly returned to my desk.

When I saw there was nothing to show that he had come, I started to eat. I had just leaned down and taken a big bite out of my sandwich. I could feel the mayonnaise oozing from the sides of my mouth, and I was slurping up a juicy slice of tomato when the elevator doors opened and in walked this gorgeous man. He was at least 6'6 or taller and a cool 200 pounds. His skin was the color of honey caramel, and his eyes were dark-chocolate brown. He looked like a well-tanned Greek god and was impeccably groomed. I almost dropped my sandwich. I tried to chew faster so I could say hello or something.

In the same deep, sultry voice I had heard before over the phone, he smiled and said, "I'll wait until you're finished."

Unnerved by this magnificent vision before my eyes and me with food stuffed in my mouth, I chewed as fast as I could, almost choking. Then I finally managed to say, "Hello, I'm sorry. May I help you?"

Again, with that deep, sultry, sexy-sounding voice, he said, "I'm Patrick Giddeons, and I have an appointment to see Kyle Simmons."

My mouth wanted to drop open, but I could not bring myself to move. I just stared at him, frozen in time. Finally, he looked down the hall towards Kyle's office, probably waiting for me to call him, but I just couldn't move. My eyes, probably as big as saucers, never left his face. I think he knew what effect he was having on me, because he stopped and *posed* right there in front of me. At that particular moment, Karan came out of her office. She saw him and said, "Hi, Patrick," in this fake, oh-I-really-like-you, how-are-you-doing sugary-sweet sort of voice.

He gallantly took her hand and kissed it, saying, "All is well when I see you, Karan."

I could have listened to that sexy voice coming from that sexy body all day long.

Patrick continued. "I dropped by because they're trying to pin something else on me now."

Karan came closer to him as he held onto her hand and gave him a fake hug. She said, "Well, you know where to come when they start in on you."

Turning to me, she said, "Have you met Nikki, our new receptionist? Well, she isn't that new any longer. Wipe your mouth, honey, you have mayonnaise dripping on the side of your mouth."

I could have died. I had felt it on my mouth when it happened, but when this Adonis walked up to my desk, I had been immobilized. All I could do was stare at him.

While they were engulfed in their conversation, everyone came out of the conference room at once, as if on cue. When Kyle saw Patrick, he came down the hall towards him, his arm stretched out, ready to shake his hand once they were close enough. He said, "Patrick, I didn't know that you were here. Nikki, I thought I asked you to let me know when he arrived."

Patrick replied, "Oh, I just walked in."

Kyle led Patrick down the hall to his office. Once in there, he called me and told me to tell everyone not to go anywhere until he finished his meeting with Patrick, and I should call them when he and Patrick were ready.

"Okay," I responded. I quickly made my phone calls. Once I did that, I ran to Karan's office.

"Why didn't you tell me he was a black god?"

She responded nonchalantly, "Different strokes for different folks. He isn't all that to me, and I wasn't sure what you would like."

"I like—I like."

"Well, he's available; he's *always* available."

"I thought he had someone—"

She interrupted, "People like Patrick are always looking for the next best thing and who knows, it could be you."

"I would sure like to try."

Karan said, "I'll feel him out and see what he thinks of you. One thing I've found out about Patrick is he doesn't hold his tongue."

"Speaking of tongues, you think he was turned off by the mayonnaise thing?"

"No, but next time be more careful."

After that, Kyle buzzed me, so I called everyone to the conference room. I waved at Tom on his way down. I waved at Robert also. They all were in the conference room for about an hour, then everyone came out except Kyle and Patrick. There faces were blank. I couldn't read any expressions at all. I hoped that everything was fine. Then when Kyle and Patrick came out of the office, they were still talking. I could hear Kyle saying that everything seemed fine, and all they had to do was to find the driver of the car.

When they got down to Karan's office, she popped out and said, "Patrick, can I talk with you before you leave?"

He smiled. "Sure, you know I'm always yours when I'm here."

She gave me a smile and a wink. Kyle stood there talking with Patrick for just a little while longer before he went back to his office. When Karan motioned Patrick into her office, I got up and ran down the hall to the ladies' room. I tried to stay in there until I thought that he had left, but I got scared because I did not transfer the phone lines so I went back. They were coming out of her office, and as I went around to my desk, I could see him checking me out. I wanted to die. How could I ask her to talk to him for me? Patrick never said anything to me. He just went to the elevator. I watched those buns leave. They were magnificent.

Once the elevator doors closed, I looked up at Karan, who was standing outside her door watching me. She raised her finger and pointed it at me, then summoned me to her office. I came in and sat down.

"What did you say to him?"

Karan smiled coyly and said, "I told him that my new person was checking him out, and she wanted to know if he was busy Saturday night."

"You *didn't* say that?"

She smirked, "I sure did—not."

I breathed a sigh of relief and laughed. "Okay, tell me the real deal."

She said, "Well, I just asked him when he was going to invite me to one of his famous parties. He has them all the time, and I never go. He said that I was welcomed anytime and to bring along my fine receptionist. He said *definitely* bring you along, and maybe we can hook up or something like that."

"Really?"

"Yeah, really, so I hope you don't have anything to do this Saturday night because we are going to his house."

I got butterflies in my stomach just thinking about it.

"What should I wear?"

"He would probably want you to wear as little as possible, but that's up to you. I'm going to wear something casual but not too revealing."

"Okay, me too."

I knew that I didn't have anything of the sort in my closet. I would have to buy something. I had not bought anything casual since I started working here. Everything was for work because work was my life. After work, I would have to go to the mall and find something, but still, I was not sure what. I asked Karan if she would take me and help me find something and she said okay. I went through the rest of the day as if I had won a million dollars. Everyone noticed, but no one really said anything except, "You sure are happy today." *Yeah, isn't life beautiful*, I thought.

After work, I caught the elevator with Karan and Joel. They had a sort of sneaky look on their face, but I didn't pay much attention to it. Karan and I went to her car. She had a nice Toyota Camry. It looked new. On the way to the mall, she said, "I kind of heard about the area you're living in. Why don't you start looking for somewhere safer to live?"

"I will, but I have just a few more bills to get caught up on first."

"You know that if you until wait next year, Kyle will co-sign for a car for you under the firm if you want. He likes to see how long the employee is going to last before he does something like that."

"Oh?"

I told her that I was not really prepared for a car yet, but that I would keep it in mind when I became financially able to afford one.

"Why do you have so many bills?"

"It's a long story. Maybe I'll tell you about it one day."

The mall that she took me to was nice, but it looked really expensive. I told her of my concerns and she said she would take me to the clearance racks. I felt a little bad by the way she said that, but I really could not afford some of the prices that I saw. We finally got to one store that I just adored, and I decided I would splurge this one time. I liked one particular outfit, but Karan picked out another. It was nice, but I thought it was a little too hootchie, but she said that it was what all the girls would be wearing and reminded me that I wanted to impress Patrick, so I bought it.

After that, we went to have drinks at one of the restaurants there, and then she took me home. Before dropping me off, she made a comment like, "Remind me to make sure I bring you home before dark next time." I smiled and said that I would. Then I got out of the car and went to my building. Stepping on the broken sidewalk, I thought, *I have really got to move.*

The next day I was on time—not too early and not late. George was already on the elevator when I got on.

"Good morning," I said.

"How are you?" he asked with a smile.

"Wonderful."

When we got off the elevator, I watched him as he walked on ahead of me. He had a sort of bounce to his step this morning. I thought things must be going fine with him. I greeted everyone I saw and checked the messages from last night. There weren't many, but I transferred them to the right person. Then I was on my way to the break room when Joel summoned me down the hall. After he went back into his office, I rolled my eyes and wondered what the problem was. Not in a hurry, I slowly walked down to the office and went in.

He said, "Will you sit down, please."

I did as he asked. He said, "I'm aware of certain activities for this Saturday night, and I want to be the one to inform you that not everyone is invited to this party of Patrick's."

I didn't say a word. He continued, "Contrary to the beliefs of many in this office, I do know what goes on around here, and I want you to know that I am watching you."

I rolled my head back and forth. "Are you finished? I have to get the coffee started, and you know the BOSS likes his coffee."

Finished with my words, I jumped up from the seat and started out the door. I was in too good of a mood today to let anyone spoil it—especially Joel.

"Wait a minute," he said, "I'm not finished."

I thought of all the days in the week, why should I have to lose my job today, only a few days before the party on Saturday. I knew I would have to talk with Kyle about Joel. I just didn't know how to. It seemed to me that they had some weird relationship going on, and I might be fired anyway, but I would have to try.

I went on to the break room and started the coffee. I took everyone theirs before I took Kyle his. I went back to the break room to get his cup when I saw Robert. He was making the hot chocolate I had bought him.

"You like it, huh?"

He turned around and said, "Oh, yeah, I thought I told you that."

I shook my head and said, "Ever since I made a fool of myself, we haven't really talked at all."

He said, "Oh, I'm sorry, I didn't mean to make such a big deal about the rides home."

"I just didn't want people talking and pointing at you, saying that you were dating your receptionist."

He said, "Well, I'm not, and what would be wrong with that if I were?"

"You know you being a lawyer and all, that wouldn't look good to your friends and co-workers."

He answered, "If that were the case, then I would not deserve such a person if I worried about what other people think."

"That's true."

He said, "So, we can call it a draw?"

"Yes, we can."

Illegal Love | 45

We stood there talking so long I had to warm Kyle's coffee in the microwave. When I went to his office, he was looking over some documents. I asked him if I could have a talk with him.

He said, "Sure, have a seat."

I closed the door and sat down.

"How is your morning going?" I asked him.

He said, "Everything is going fine."

"I think that I have problem," I said.

He put his document down and turned towards me, giving me his full attention. "What do you mean?"

"It's Joel."

He leaned back and said, "Oh?

"Nikki, don't take Joel too personally. He's just hard like that. Things here aren't going the way he thought they would and sometimes, he takes that out on the people who he feels have less responsibility than he does. Just ask Karan. She'll tell you he's a little hard to get along with."

"Well, I don't think I'll be here for years if he keeps talking to me the way that he does."

He said, "Oh, I see. Well, don't go quitting on me. I need you. Tell you what, I'll have a talk with him."

"Thank you."

As I got up to leave the office, he said, "You know that Patrick is having a party, and that means *everyone* in the office is invited."

He continued, "And you know if you need a ride, I could come by and pick you up."

"Thanks, but I'm going to ride with Karan."

"OK, I'll see you there."

I walked out of the office and had a pretty pleased look on my face. It wasn't easy, but I had stood up for myself. It was a beginning. I walked down the hall with a smile of self-assurance. When I passed Karan's office, she asked me to come in. I came in, still wearing that look of having maimed Goliath.

When I sat down, she asked, "What's with you?"

"I just got a victory over Joel," I smiled.

She said, "Oh, my God, what happened?"

I told her what Joel had done and then what I did by talking with Kyle.

She said, "I just want to say that I hope it works out, but it has never worked with any of the other temps before."

"Yes, but I'm not a temp anymore."

She replied, "Yes, but you, still like me, are just a lowly employee."

"No, not like you, and I will not be treated any kind of way by anyone. I know what it's like to be treated like nothing, and I won't be treated like that anymore."

She said, "Well, I hope that your cause is validated."

I rose to go back to my desk. When I got there, I waited for the mail to arrive. Shortly after it came, I started sorting it when in walked Ms. Buffy. I rolled my eyes up in my head and politely asked, "How may I help you?"

"George, please."

"Just a moment." I rang his office, and he ran out of it to greet her. I thought, *Well, it's back on again*. She gave me a look and then said, "Darling, I came as soon as you called."

I felt this was for my benefit. She sashayed over to him, and they went into his office and closed the door. Karan came to her door and said, "See what I told you?"

"Yeah," I replied and threw up my hands.

She laughed, I laughed, and then she went back into her office. I finished sorting the mail and got ready to take it to the offices. Just at that moment, Patrick walked through the door. I froze. He had been in yesterday, and I didn't think he would have to come back to the office again this week.

He said, "Hi, how are you?"

"Fine," I stammered.

He said, "I know that, but how are you doing?"

I smiled, relaxed a bit, and said, "I'm okay, how may I help you today?"

He said, "Is Kyle in?"

"Yes, can you wait for a minute?"

I called Kyle and he asked me, "Why is he here?"

"I don't know."

He instructed me to tell him he'd be right there.

Then I told Patrick that Kyle was on his way. While he waited, I asked, "How are things going with your party?"

He looked at me funny. I wondered if maybe I should not have said that. I was just trying to make some small talk, but I think that I was annoying him. He said that everything was going okay and went to sit down. Just then, Kyle came down the hall. They shook hands, and I caught a little bit of what they were discussing. Patrick told Kyle that something had come up, and he needed to discuss it with him.

Kyle said, "Well, let's talk about it in my office."

Shortly after the door closed, Kyle buzzed me and asked me to have Robert come down to his office immediately. I called Robert, gave him the message, and he wanted to know if I knew what was happening.

Shortly after that, he came rushing down the hall. He winked at me as he passed by. I put my hands over my eyes and shook my head. I wondered what happened now. Of course, Karan stuck her head out of the door and asked if Patrick was back.

"Yes," I said.

Her eyebrows shot up in the air, and she made a funny little thing with her mouth. I shrugged my shoulders as to say I didn't know what was going on. She shook her head then went back to her office.

After the mail came and I had sorted everything, I went to deliver it. Even though I felt I had a victory this morning when I discussed Joel's behavior with Kyle, when I got down to Joel's office, I dreaded knocking on the door, but I did. He didn't say anything to me; as a matter of fact, he didn't even look up when I walked into the office. I put his mail down and left, then knocked on Kyle's door. He told me to enter, and I held up his mail.

"Please bring it back later."

I closed his door and went down to Karan's office. Her door was open, and she motioned me in and told me to close the door. I took a seat. She asked me why Patrick came back today, then said,

"Well, maybe his alibi isn't as tight as he needs it to be."

"Really?" I replied. "What happened?"

"Well, I heard that the girl might not want to testify on his behalf anymore."

"No way," I said.

She shook her head.

"How do you know?" I asked.

"Who do you think makes all the calls around here for appointments, and who do you think types up all the legal documents? Me, that's who. I know everything about this place and their clients."

She continued, "I called the woman yesterday after Patrick had left to make an appointment with her to take a statement, and she told me that I would need to talk with her lawyer. When I told Kyle that, he was not too pleased."

"So do you think Kyle knew that Patrick was coming in today, because he surely seemed caught off guard when I told him he was here?"

"Maybe, I don't know, but I told you that boy is nothing but trouble."

I got up to leave the office. "Do you think I should go to the party?"

She said, "That's up to you, I was only going because of you."

I told her that I'd think about it. When I got back to my desk, George and Buffy were just coming out of his office. They looked like two lovebirds. I could have puked, but I had been warned. Before she walked out of the door, she turned around and waved good-bye to me. I waved back. I didn't want George to think I didn't like his fiancée.

After a while, Robert came out of Kyle's office and shortly thereafter, Kyle and Patrick came out. They talked a little on the way down the hall and then stopped in front of my desk.

Kyle said to him, "I'll see you tomorrow."

Patrick looked at me and said, "You're going come to, pretty lady, aren't you?"

"You bet."

Kyle looked at me and smiled. Patrick left, and I went on with my day. TGIF. I loved my job, but thank God it was Friday.

On Saturday, I was waiting on Karan to come around 6 P.M. She had called earlier to say that she would be here by 6:00, so that we could get to the party when Kyle and the other bunch arrived. I felt a little uncomfortable in the outfit I had on, but Karan had assured me that everything would be fine. I waited. She finally got here around 6:45. She called from the car to say that she was downstairs and that she hoped I was ready because she was not leaving her car out there.

"I'm on my way down," I replied.

When I got to the car, I couldn't believe how she was dressed. She looked really nice. She had on long silk pants with a silk blouse—nothing like what she had picked out for me to wear. I really felt underdressed. As a matter of fact, I felt like a street hooker next to her.

"Don't you think I should go up and change? I think that my skirt might be a little short and much too tight," I said.

She smiled, "Oh, no, Nikki, you look gorgeous. If you are referring to my attire, I just don't have the body like you do, so I can't wear just anything."

I looked at her trying to believe her. We drove off. On the way there, she stopped at the gas station and bought some cigarettes. I didn't know that she smoked.

She said, "No one else does either. I just do it on the weekends. It's not a habit or anything."

I thought there is so much I don't know about the woman that I work with every day. We drove on to Patrick's house. When we got there, there were plenty of cars already parked. We found a place to park, then we went inside. The house was huge. It looked to me to be the size of my whole apartment building. Some girl greeted us at the door; she was dressed like me. I started feeling a little less uncomfortable. Music blasted from somewhere inside, but I couldn't tell from where. The ceiling looked to be 50 feet tall. Everything was beautiful. I thought Patrick must surely have good taste.

Karan and I went looking to see if any of the guys from the office had arrived. After meandering all through the magnificent house, we didn't see them, so we went downstairs to look for something to munch on. We found it. Tables were set up with all kinds of food. Chicken, shrimp, lobster, crab, salads, pasta, and fruit trays. Everything you thought you might want to eat, he had it. We had just fixed a little something to nibble on, and I was putting it in my mouth when Patrick spotted us. He came over. I dropped my piece of chicken and tried to hurry up and chew what was already in my mouth.

He said, "Hey, girls, what's up?"

Karan said, "I love your parties. They are always the best."

He said, "Yeah ..."

I was trying desperately to swallow by this point. He looked over at me swallowing and said, "I keep catching you like this."

I nodded my head as the last of it went down.

"Yeah, we have to stop meeting in these awkward situations," I laughed.

He asked, "Are the guys here yet?"

Karan answered, "We haven't seen them."

"Okay, when you do, tell Kyle I'm looking for him," then he drifted off to meet some other guests.

I thought, *Well, that was a real brush-off.* I looked at Karan, and she must have been reading my thoughts because she said, "Honey, don't take it personally. He has a lot of guests to see to."

"Yeah, you're right."

Then she saw someone that she knew and told me to wait here for a minute. I pointed over to an empty spot on the sofa were I would be sitting. I must have sat over there for an hour waiting on her to come back. I was holding my plate that whole time. I didn't want to put it down on his lovely furniture, so I finally got up to go look for a garbage can. I put the almost-empty plate with chicken bones still on it in the trash and turned around. To my surprise—and horror—there was my ex standing no less than 2 feet away from me. He was talking with some girls and probably filling their heads with some lies. I tried to walk away before he saw me, but I was too late. He looked up and our eyes met. At first, his expression scared me, then he put this really big smile on his face. I could see him telling his crowd that he would be back. I still tried to run.

He said loudly, "Nikki, Nikki Salime."

I stopped. It was too late. I took a deep breath and turned around. I tried to smile, but I think I only showed him the fear that I had inside.

He said, "Oh, baby, why you looking like that?"

"Looking like what?"

He said, "Like you have something to fear from me."

He put his hands on my head and slid them over my face, cupping my chin with his palm. He said, "I would never hurt you."

Then he kissed me on my cheek. I thought tears would come out of my eyes.

He said, "Baby, where have you been? Damn, you still look good."

I stood there, still not being able to say anything. He continued, "Are you going to talk to me or what?"

"Oh, yeah ... I um ..."

By this time, Karan was approaching. I took this opportunity to excuse myself and said that I'd catch up with him later. Then I ran past him and almost fell into Karan's arms. She said, "Are you all right? You look like you've seen a ghost."

Illegal Love | 51

"No, just someone I used to know."

She said, "Here?"

I looked at her strangely and said, "Yes, here."

She said, "Well, where are they? Are you going to introduce them to me?"

"You wouldn't want to meet them."

I turned her around to walk the other way. I hoped that he didn't see her. She said, "Well, the guys are finally here."

"Good, let's go find them."

We went out by the pool. There was Kyle, with who I assumed was his wife. George was with Buffy, of course. Tom was with his wife, who, by the way, was prettier than I expected. Joel was by himself, of course. Who would go out with him? And Robert was alone. I walked over with Karan, and Joel's eyes almost popped out of his head. Actually, they all stared at me. I knew I shouldn't have worn this outfit. I felt really uncomfortable as Kyle introduced me to everyone. I tried not to show it, but I think that Robert noticed. He came over and stood by me. Soon, everyone left the area and started mingling. Robert and I started talking, and I told him that I wasn't feeling well, that I was going to find Karan to see if she would take me home.

He said, "If you want me to, I'll take you home."

"Are you sure?"

He said, "Yes, I really didn't want to be here anyway."

"Well, I still need to let Karan know that I'm going. I'll meet you at the front door."

I started looking for her, then I saw that she was with Joel. I didn't want to go over near him but I had come with her and I didn't want her to worry. I walked up to them and said, "Excuse me, Karan."

She turned around and said, "Hey, sweetie."

"I'm not feeling well, and I think I need to leave."

She said, "Oh, but everything is just getting going."

"I know, and you can stay. I've found a ride."

She said, "Oh, really?"

Joel said, "I'm sure—with that outfit on."

I tensed up a bit. I expected something, but much sooner than now. Ignoring him, I turned back to Karan and said, "Anyway, I just wanted to let you know that I was leaving."

She said, "Well, I hope you feel better. I'm sure Patrick will miss you."

I thought not, but said, "Well, tell him that I'll see him at the office."

She said, "Okay. Bye."

I walked towards the door. There he was again. *Damned, I thought I'd be able to leave without seeing him.* I looked for Robert over by the door, but he wasn't there, and here was my worst nightmare coming closer to me. I looked again and there was Patrick coming over *with* him. My nightmare said, "Hey, Pat, you know this girl?"

Patrick said, "Yeah, but when I first saw her, she didn't look this fine."

He said, "Yeah, she was always surprising me too. This is an old friend of mine, Nikki," and then he put his arms around me.

I nearly shrank.

The nightmare spoke again. "Yeah, Nikki and me used to live together—before she left me."

Patrick said, "Yeah? I heard this guy can be murder to live with."

I thought to myself that murder was almost right, at least, that's what he almost did to me.

"I'm sorry I have to leave. I'm not feeling well."

Patrick said, "Well, I'm glad that you came, and I hope that you feel better."

Then he left, but, oh, not the nightmare. He stayed there with his arm tight around me.

"Well, it has been nice seeing you again, but I don't feel well, and my ride is waiting for me."

He said, "Now, don't rush off." Then his grip on me got tighter.

"I'll scream, I promise you that."

He loosened up a little and said, "For what? Because I'm hugging you? I'm just trying to show you love."

"I have to go."

He moved his arm and said, "Okay, I'll catch you later. I see that my boy knows how to get in touch with you, and I *will* see you later."

The way he said that scared me to death. I thought that I had gotten over my fear of him, but just seeing him again just for these brief moments made it all come back. I looked at him and almost ran to the door.

When I got outside, Robert was in front of the house in the car. I wondered how long he had been there waiting for me. I jumped in the car and almost burst into tears.

He said, "What's wrong?"

"I can't talk about it. I just need to get home."

"I don't think that's what you need to do."

He drove off, but kept looking over at me. Then he told me there were some napkins in the glove compartment if I needed one. After I got myself together, he asked if I wanted to go and get a drink, that maybe if I talked it out, I might feel better. I said that I would take the drink, but I did not feel like talking it out. He drove to a bar that was in between my place and his. It was nice, quiet, and dark. That was fine with me, because right now, the last thing I wanted was to see someone else I knew. We ordered and waited for the drinks to come. He stared at me for a while, and then he said, "Are you sure you don't want to talk about it?"

"Yes, I'm sure."

"I'll respect your wishes then."

Our drinks came, and I downed mine. I thought that it would help the pain that was filling my body. I called the waitress over for another one.

He said, "You really don't feel good, do you?"

I didn't say anything. When my second drink came, I downed it. Then I ordered another one. He was still sipping on his first one. He didn't question what I was doing, he just sat there with me. By now, I was lit.

"Why don't you have someone special in your life? What's wrong with you?" I suddenly asked him, and I think I caught him off guard with those questions.

He looked at me and said, "I thought we were here for *you*."

"Well, we can be here for both of us." Then I laughed. I felt that he knew I was not being myself, but I couldn't tell. The whole room was spinning by now. In a slurred, unrecognizable voice, I persisted, "Well, why aren't you attached? Did you know that you are one of the most sought-after males in our building?"

He just sat there.

"Am I talking too much?"

Still he said nothing. My drink came, and I downed it. I ordered another. I think I saw him tell the waitress no, but I was not sure, not in this state anyway. I pointed my finger at him and said, "Do you know that you are too attractive not to be taken?"

Then he said, "Do you know that you are too attractive to be acting like this?"

"Oh, but you are so wrong. I am not attractive. I have scars—deep scars."

"Well, getting drunk isn't going to help you at all."

"It's better than facing the truth sometimes."

"I think we should go."

"Oh no, you are a party pooper. I'm just now having fun. Is that why you don't have anyone? Because you're a party booper? Oh, I mean pooper, or maybe I do mean booper."

He laughed and said, "You're drunk."

"Yes, but not drunk enough."

He came over to my side and said, "Let's go."

"But, darling, you haven't finished your drink."

I reached over and drank it. He shook his head. He left the money on the table for the waitress, and we went back to the car. He said, "You're going to have to tell me which apartment you live in."

"No."

"What?"

"No, I don't want to go home."

"But, Nikki, you need to get to bed and sleep this off."

"Good, then take me to your bed."

"What?"

I looked at him, then I smiled. "Oh, are you afraid of the little girly?"

He drove off. I couldn't tell where I was. All I knew was that I was riding. We finally got into a parking garage, and I figured he had taken me back to the office.

"I don't want to go to work."

He didn't say anything. He just came over to my side of the car and opened the door. He had to help me out because by now, I couldn't feel my legs. He had me lean on him to help me walk.

"You're such a gentleman."

"Thanks, but if you had been more of a lady, I wouldn't have to do this."

"Well, don't get mad. I just gave you a compliment."

He took me over to the elevator and punched in a code. When it came, I didn't want to get on it. It went back up.

"Now, Nikki, this is the only way I can get you upstairs."

"I don't want to go to work."

"This is my building. You are not going to work."

"Oh?"

Then he punched in the code again. The elevator came back. We went up to the lobby, and then we had to get out to go to some more elevators. He punched a number again, and we went zooming up. When the elevator stopped, there was plush carpeting on the floor, just like in a hotel.

"You live in a hotel? You make too much money to be living in a hotel."

"This is not a hotel."

"Well, my apartment does not have carpeting in the lobby."

We walked a couple of doors down, then he leaned me up against the wall. After opening the door, he grabbed me again. It was dark. He touched a button as we walked through the door, and the lights came on.

"Too bright! Pleassse, too bright," I protested. He did something and immediately, the lights dimmed. Then he walked me down a hall and into a room. He placed me on the bed, and then went to get something. What he came back with was a set of his jammies.

"Here, put these on."

"You do it."

He said sternly, "Nikki, please put these on!"

When I started taking off my blouse, he left the room. I somehow got undressed and managed to put on his things.

In a seductive voice I said, "Are you coming to bed now?"

"No, go to sleep."

He came in and got my clothes.

"I don't want to go to sleep. Come talk with me please."

He came in and sat by the bed and then he talked to me until I feel asleep.

When I woke up, my head was killing me and I didn't know where I was. I just stared up at the ceiling thinking I must be in Patrick's bed, but I thought that I had left with someone. I kept looking around, but I couldn't figure it out. I turned from left to right and all it really did was to make my head swim more. Then I felt stomach pain, like when it isn't going to agree with you. I got up and looked for the bathroom. Spotting it, I ran into it just in time, kneeled over the toilet, and let out everything I had eaten the previous night. I leaned to the side. Then I vomited again. I wanted to cry, but I thought that would only make it worse. After that, I heard someone coming. I got scared and drew up in a ball.

It was Robert, but what was he doing here?

"Did that make you feel any better?"

"No. Where am I?"

"You're at my place."

"Why?" Then I leaned back over the toilet.

"That's why."

I held my stomach and shook my head. He gave me a wet washrag. It was cold.

"Put this on the back of your neck."

It made me feel a little better.

"There's a new toothbrush in that drawer on the sink. Use it and then get back in bed."

I tried to get up, but my legs were weak. He came over and helped me. I leaned over the sink, got the toothbrush, and brushed my teeth. With every stroke, I thought I would puke again. Finally, all cleaned up, he took me back over to the bed. It was nice and soft, with a lovely comforter on it. I tried to look around again but still could not grasp anything. He came in with a small garbage can and then a bowl with ice in it.

"If you got sick, throw up in the garbage can next time. I don't want you missing the toilet bowl. The ice is for your head. It'll help your headache."

"What are you going to do?"

"I'll be in the other room if you need me."

I lay there and thought that I could probably kiss my job good-bye. I couldn't remember much, but the one thing I did remember was that I had seen my nightmare in hi-def living color and I was afraid. He said that he would be trying to get in touch with me, and that scared the shit out of me. The thought of it made me puke again. I leaned over the garbage can and let loose. After I finished, I called Robert, and he came quickly.

"What's wrong?"

"I need something to wipe my mouth with."

"I'm sorry; I should have brought you a towel or something."

"Can I ask you something?"

"Yeah, sure. What?"

"Did we do anything last night?"

He laughed and said, "No, why?"

"Well, before, I thought that you were a gentleman, but now I know for sure. Can I ask you something else?"

"Shoot."

"How bad was I last night?"

"Worse than you want to know."

I turned my head around. I could have died right there. Boy, would this be news around the office! I'd never hear the end of it, and Karan would eat this up. I think Robert knew what I was thinking.

"You don't have to worry; this will not go past this house unless *you* tell someone yourself."

I turned back towards him. "Why are you being so nice to me?"

"Well, it isn't anyone's business in the first place, and the second place is that something or some*one* at that party last night scared you into this, and that makes me mad."

He looked at me as if hoping that I would say something about it, but I didn't. He turned back around and went into the bathroom. After a moment, he came out with a washcloth and laid it on the night table next to me. I leaned over and got it and wiped my mouth, hoping that he didn't think that I was disgusting or anything. He asked me if I was hungry. I wasn't, and anyway, I told him that I don't think that I could hold anything down right now. He shook his head in agreement and started to walk out of the room, but I called him back.

"One day I might be able to tell you about last night, but right now, I feel that I have shattered your image of me enough."

"You still don't understand me, do you?"

Then he walked out of the room. I felt terrible, not just the hangover but from the sight of my ex last night and then acting the way I did with Robert afterwards, and of course, this morning. I ached inside and out. All day I drifted in and out of sleep, and when I was awake, I was sick. I lay there until 3:00 or so then I finally got up and went into the living room. It was set up very nice. I thought he must have paid a decorator a lot of money to make his house this comfortable and elegant at the same time. Robert was sitting on the sofa going over some paperwork. I cleared my throat.

"I heard you when you got up."

"You work on the weekends too?"

"I like what I do, and I do it well, and sometimes it takes more than 9–5, Monday–Friday."

"Sure, whatever rocks your boat, but if you had a woman, you wouldn't be working so much on the weekend."

He turned and looked at me. I could tell I had angered him.

"I want to say this to you, and I want to say it to you just once. I don't pay attention to gossip about other people, and I don't want to hear about the gossip that is spread about me."

"I'm sorry, it's just everyone in the building knows about your breakup but me, and I was just saying that maybe you shouldn't dwell on it."

He turned back around and focused on his work once again. At that moment, he could have thrown last night into my face, but being the gentleman he was, I don't think it even crossed his mind. I walked around for a little bit, then I came and sank on the couch next to him. It was leather, but it was so soft. I had always thought that leather was hard and that when you sat on it, it made a sort of crunchy sound, but not this. It was smooth as I rubbed it. He turned and looked at me with a smile on his face. I looked all around.

"You must have paid a pretty penny to have someone do this for you."

"Do what for me?"

"You know, decorate this place for you."

"What makes you think that I paid someone to do this for me?"

"Because no man has taste this good unless he's gay." I raised an eyebrow and looked questioning his way.

"I am *not* gay, and my taste is excellent."

"Okay, so when I move, you're going to hook me up too, right? But you know I can't afford the kind of stuff that you have, so it will have to be on the down low."

"Sure, if you want."

"Yeah, you say that now, but when the time comes, I probably won't be able to find you."

"Sure you will. I'll be in the office down the hall."

"Yeah, if I have a job by then."

"Why do you doubt yourself so much?"

"Did you see what I had on last night? I don't know how I let Karan talk me into wearing such an outfit."

He didn't say anything. He just turned back to what he was doing with his work.

"What did I say wrong?"

He said nothing.

"I know that I said something wrong, because you didn't respond."

"You shouldn't let other people influence you so much."

"I know, but I wanted to look good, and I thought that her taste was better than mine."

He didn't say anything, but I looked at him, hoping that he would. He kept working. I said, "So are you hungry?"

"A little."

"Well, if I cooked, I would feed us both, but since I don't, I'll be willing to treat you to a late lunch."

"Honestly, I don't really feel like going anywhere right now, but if you give me a minute, I'll let you help me fix us something."

I sat back and said, "Cool, it's your place."

He continued to work on the documents in front of him for a little while. I got up and went to freshen up in the bathroom, then remembering what I had been doing all morning, I cleaned up my mess around his bed. By the time I finished, he was ready.

"Okay, chef boy-r-dee, what are we having?"

"Just something I like to fix for myself sometimes, and I hope that you will like too."

He got out the wok and some olive oil. Then he took out some chicken, lettuce, tomatoes, onion, bell peppers, and some pita bread. As he started cooking the chicken, he had me chop the vegetables, then he threw the onions and bell peppers in the wok. It smelled good, but at the same time, my stomach seemed like it wanted to act up. Nevertheless, I didn't let that stop me. We were there working side by side, and it was really nice. He gave me bowls to put the rest of the vegetables in and then handed me some plates for the table. I set up everything and waited for him to sit down. Soon, everything was ready but Robert. He had to clean the kitchen before he came. I thought that was very neat of him. As I looked around, I noticed that everything was very neat. It looked almost like no one lived here at all. I thought I probably could eat on his floor.

We had tea considering my last episode with alcohol. The food was delicious. We ate, then did the dishes together. I couldn't understand why we did the dishes by hand when he had a beautiful dishwasher there, but I didn't ask questions. I was just thankful for the meal. It was getting late, and he asked if I was ready to go home.

I wanted to say no but instead said, "Sure."

Maybe he was trying to get rid of me, and maybe it was just late. He took me to his closet.

"I washed your things."

"Thanks."

I got dressed, and we left. As we entered the hallway outside his apartment, I commented on how neat it looked and how it reminded me of a hotel.

"Yeah, you said that last night."

I knew it was a joke, but I was a little sensitive about my behavior from the previous night, so I just shrugged it off.

"I like it too. It's one of the reasons I took the apartment."

We rode down to the lobby and then took another elevator to his car. I confessed that I didn't remember any of it. He said he was not surprised; he almost had to carry me up. I shook my head in disbelief.

"I am so sorry."

"No problem, but next time, the person might not be as kind as I was, and maybe you should rethink getting that drunk again."

"Hopefully it won't happen again."

We drove the couple of blocks to my house in silence. When he parked in front of my place, I leaned over and kissed him on the cheek.

"Thanks for everything."

He was blushing, and that made me smile. I got of the car and went home.

Chapter 6

Monday morning arrived, and I came in early with bells on. I had hoped that my party outfit would not be the topic of discussion today, but I did anticipate something harsh from Joel. However, seeing how I felt right now, I would just let it slide off. I went to my desk, checked the messages from the weekend, and transferred all the calls. I then went into the break room to start the coffee. I had also brought Robert a little thank you bag of hot chocolate. I was hoping that he would already be in, but I didn't see his office door open when I came down the hall. The buzz of Monday morning started with everyone walking through the door having something to say about my outfit. First, there was George.

"I didn't know you had it in you, girl."

"Good morning, George."

Second, there was Tom.

"Nice outfit Saturday."

"Good morning, Tom." I said it with a smile.

Third, there was Joel.

"I'm glad you dress better for work."

"Good morning, Joel."

But under my breath, the F-you word was trying to come out.

Fourth, there was Kyle. He came through the door with a grin on his face like the Lord himself had spoken to him. He said, "Now, *that* is what I'm talking about. You really surprised me on Saturday."

Then he leaned on the counter close to me and said, "When can I take you out, and will you wear that outfit for me?"

61

62 | Felicia Truttier

I tried to play it off by saying, "Kyle, you are so crazy." Luckily, Robert walked through the door just in time. Kyle straightened up.

"I'll talk with you later about that," he said.

Robert started down the hall towards his office. I got up and followed.

"So, what has the feedback been on your outfit?"

"Oh, just the usual mess."

He smiled, and I smiled back at him.

"How's your head?"

"It's wonderful."

"I know that, but how is the hangover part?"

"Oh, it was fine by the time I left your apartment."

"If I had known that, I would have let you stay longer. I thought you needed some time to get ready for today."

"Don't tell me stuff you are not willing to back up."

"I never say anything I'm not willing to back up. That's why I became a lawyer."

With that, he went into his office. I thought to myself, now *that* was a come-on. I took everyone's coffee around, but when I got to Robert's office, I thought I might just be a little bold. I tapped on the door.

"Come in."

When I went into his office, I thought that he looked extra handsome today. He was tall, about 6 foot 3 or 4, weighed about 190, and was very well cut. I could tell that from the T-shirt he had on yesterday. He was well-groomed, and he wore a beard that lined his face. It was trimmed low, not bushy. He always looked good, but today, he looked sexier than usual. He had his jacket off, and I noticed he wore suspenders. I thought to myself, *Does he always wear suspenders, and I just haven't paid attention? Why am I paying so much attention today?* I walked over to his desk with his chocolate.

"You didn't have to do this; I still have a little bit left."

"Yeah, I figured that, but a little bit is not enough for someone who took care of me so well this weekend."

"It wasn't a problem."

"Maybe I should get plastered every weekend then."

He looked up at me in confusion and said, "Why would you want to do that?"

"Well, then you would have to take care of me."

I put the mug on his desk and started out of the office.

Illegal Love | 63

"Nikki."

I turned around. "Yes, Robert?" I said in a sultry way.

"You don't have to act like that you know."

"Like what?"

"Well, like that dress you had on the other night. I liked you just fine before you wore it."

Quite embarrassed, I walked out of his office and went down the hall thinking that Robert normally would not be flirting with me. That was more Kyle's style. When I got to my desk, I noticed that Karan was still not in. I went down to Kyle's office to see if she had called in and knocked on the door.

"Come in."

"Kyle, did Karan call in today?"

"Not that I know of, but she usually does if she comes in late."

"Oh, I was just worried; she has never been out since I've been here."

"No, she usually doesn't take days off unless something important comes up, but I'm sure it's nothing, and now, can we get back to *us*?"

"Sir, did you hear that?"

"What?"

"Hold that thought; I hear the phones."

I ran out of the office as if I was trying to catch the line, and I almost ran into Karan.

"Good morning, sleepyhead."

"Where are you running to, or might I ask, who are you running *from*?"

"Neither one; I thought I heard the phones."

"Uh-huh."

She went into her office, and I followed. Jokingly I said, "And why are *you* late this morning?"

She looked at me with a raised eyebrow. Then she said, "If you must know, I was downstairs talking with Niyokia, telling her about the party."

"Oh."

"And did you know that it was still going on Sunday?"

In a dry tone I said, "No, I didn't know that."

"Yeah, Patrick's parties are usually like that."

I shrugged my shoulders. I was no longer interested in Patrick, especially now that I knew what kind of friends he had.

"Yeah, I stayed there pretty late. It seems Patrick needed my advice on something, and we ended up talking most of the night."

I thought to myself that Patrick didn't seem like the type of person that could hold a conversation for longer than 10 minutes, so how could he talk to anyone *all night*?

"Well, that's good; it sounds like you two really hit it off."

"Yeah, I even went back on Sunday."

I didn't say anything like she wanted me to. I thought that she was trying to see if I would get mad, but I didn't. There was nothing for me to get upset about, because he wasn't my man, and after this weekend, I didn't want him to be.

"Well, I'll bring your coffee in."

I turned and walked out of the office. I knew that this was going to be an interesting day. The mail came, and I sorted it and answered the phones. Later during the day around lunchtime, guess who shows up? No one other than my dearest friend, Buffy, who, of course, commented on my outfit from the party Saturday night. She came up to the desk with this sneaky little grin on her face.

"Is George in?"

"I'll check for you."

I paged his office, and he didn't answer. "No, he isn't answering his phone."

"I'll wait."

But before she went to have a seat, she smirked, "I saw who you truly are the other night. That must've been the way you came in to interview with Kyle."

I almost blew up. How dare she imply that I would try to get a job based on how my body looked! I grabbed the mail and took it to the various offices. When I got to George's office, I just went in. I thought that he wasn't in, but to my surprise, there he was in a lip-lock with some woman. I dropped everything.

"Oh, I am *so* sorry."

He ran over to help me.

"I'm so sorry," I repeated again, "but you didn't answer your phone."

He didn't say anything. I whispered to him that Buffy was outside waiting on him. He looked at me.

"You have *not* seen me," he informed me.

I wanted to bellow out the loudest laugh I could, but I held it inside. We picked up the mail, and I went back to my desk to re-sort it. When I got there, Buffy looked up at me with a stupid grin on her face and as I re-sorted everything, I just shook my head and smiled very broadly. I wanted to say something so bad. I went down to Tom's office and gave him his mail.

"I, I, I hope that I, I, I didn't offend you earlier."

"No, Tom, you didn't."

He smiled. "But you di, di, did look ni, ni, nice."

"Thank you, Tom."

I turned around. "Your wife was beautiful."

"Thank you. people al, al, always ask her what di, di, did she see in, in, in me."

I walked out and knocked on Robert's door. When I came in, he was just sitting there, looking good as ever. I tried not to stare as I quickly went to put his mail on his desk.

"Is something wrong?"

"No, not really."

"Well, if not really, then what really?"

I looked up at the ceiling. "Well, earlier today, I thought that you were sort of making a pass at me. Then I caught myself making a pass back at you, but then I found myself looking like a fool."

"Oh."

I stood there thinking he had better say something besides "Oh," but he didn't.

"So, well, were you?"

He chuckled, "Yes, I think I was."

I stood *real* still. Had he just said *yes*? I smiled and said, "Well, do you want to go to lunch?"

He mocked me by saying, "And start rumors that I might be interested in a lowly receptionist?"

"Okay, I deserve that. Well, would you like to go to lunch? I'll pay."

"Oh, wow, you have offered twice in a row. I must accept it before it becomes null and void."

"Good, then it's a date."

I turned around with a little twist. I was proud of myself for not being too much of a woose. Then I went back to my desk, Buffy was still there. I put my hands over my face and rubbed it a couple of times.

I hoped that would make her disappear, but it didn't. She was still there when I looked up. I leaned back in my chair, raised my eyebrows, and said, "Buffy, I don't think George will be back today."

"Really, and how do you know that? Did he call? I haven't heard the phone ring."

I shook my head. "Never mind."

She sat there. Robert called and said that we would have to do lunch another day because he had to go see a client, but that he would probably be back in time to take me home.

"Okay."

It took Buffy another 3 hours as I did my work before she left. George and the mystery woman never came out of the office. Finally, the end of the day came, and Robert had still not gotten back. Everyone started leaving, and I was trying to hang around. Then Kyle came out of his office.

"Do you need a ride home?"

"No, I'm waiting on someone."

"Who?"

"Oh, one of the girls from the 6th floor. She lives near me."

"Ah, I thought you were trying to sneak in some overtime."

I pretended to laugh at the humorless joke.

"I'll talk with you tomorrow."

I waved good-bye as he got onto the elevator. A little time passed and still, Robert did not show up nor did he call, so I went downstairs to wait on my bus. He was right there waiting for me. I thought I would burst just from the sight of him as I ran to the car.

He said, "What took you so long?"

I told him that I had been upstairs waiting on him.

"Oh, I'm sorry, I should have called. I want to take you someplace."

"I go where you go," I smiled.

"One of the reasons I was late is because I went to see an old client of mine who owns some apartment complexes."

I didn't say anything.

"I talked to him, and he gave me a couple of keys so that I could go and look at them."

"Are you planning to move?"

He sighed, "No, it's for you."

"I'm not a welfare case. I know that you're only trying to help, but sometimes people can go too far. You don't have to treat me like charity."

"I promise you that I won't do that, but I won't lie and say that I like where you're living. I think that you should be in a safer environment. Now, do you at least want to go and see them?"

I really did want to see them so I said yes, and we took off.

There were three, and all were beautiful. I really liked one in particular, and I think that Robert knew it. He pointed out of the bay window in the living room to show me how close everything was to its location. I would be close to the grocery store and a wonderful little shopping plaza. I really loved it.

"I can't afford this."

"I promise you, you can afford this."

"How do you know?"

"Because it will cost you exactly the same amount that you are paying now."

"But you don't know what I am paying now."

"It doesn't matter. I've already talked with Mr. Robbins, and he'll rent it to you for what you are paying now."

I ran over to him and hugged him, but his time when I went to kiss him, I made sure it was on the lips. He kissed me back but then pushed me away very quickly.

"What's wrong?"

"I'm only doing this because I think that you're a nice person and you live in a crummy neighborhood, and not because I want something from you."

"I know that."

"Good."

Then I got closer to him and kissed him again. This time, he kissed me back. It was nice and long. When we stopped, I said, "I don't know if I want to live this far away from you."

"Well, if you had loved the second apartment that we saw just as much, you would have been only one block away from me on the other end."

"Oh."

As we got ready to leave, he said, "Mr. Robbins will be calling you tomorrow to talk with you about the apartment. Just tell him which

68 | Felicia Truttier

one you want. You don't have to go through a credit check or pay any deposits. Let him know when you want to move in and do it."

I hugged him again, but this time I did not kiss him. Then he took me home.

The next morning I think that I got to work way too early. I don't even remember people coming in the building when I got there. I did my usual, checked the messages, made the coffee, and waited on the crew. Everyone came in their usual selves. When George arrived, he immediately asked me into his office. I thought, okay, this is it, the big speech about what I had seen yesterday and to just forget about it. I went in already knowing what I was going to say to that. He asked me to sit down, and I did. Then he started.

"Well, Nikki, you haven't been here long, but you know the trouble that Buffy and I have gone through already."

I nodded my head in response.

"What you don't know is this has been going on for years, and sometimes a person gets tired of fighting and hearing about how someone is going to change. Well, I am that person now. I know that many people will not believe this, but it is really over with Buffy and me."

My eyes were wide with this information.

"But she is persistent, and she will come up here and wait to see if I have forgiven her once again. Nikki, I'm asking you to make sure she doesn't waste anymore of her time."

I thought, *Oh, no, he is not going to make me the bad guy on this.*

"If I have to, I will try to get her stopped before she makes it up this far, but she is devious. She would even climb stairs to get up here."

I thought, *Yeah, and you two will be back together in a couple of days, and I will look like the fool again.*

"Excuse me, sir, but have you told Buffy that you two are not together anymore?"

"Well, no, but I will be talking with her soon."

"George, it is not my job to be in the middle of situations such as this, and I think it's best that I stay out of it until you have had your little talk with her."

"I understand. Well, that's all. I think I have made the point clear."

I wondered how he could be an effective lawyer if he can't even break up with his girlfriend.

Illegal Love | 69

"Is there anything else?"

"No."

I left his office, wondering what I had gotten myself into. Here I was in an office full of babies, not to mention Karan and her lies and staying on the phone, not doing any work, just a power hungry wannabe. Speak of the devil, who waltzed off the elevator in what appeared to be a new outfit, saying that she believed that Patrick was coming into the office today and that she wanted to look her best?

"When he gets here let me know," she said.

"Okay."

I went to my desk. I thought if anything else happened, I would need a drink of coffee myself. Then the phones started ringing, and they kept on ringing. Mr. Robbins eventually called, and I told him I would call him back just as soon as I could. The guys were in and out all day, mostly out, but every now and then, I would catch a glimpse of one of them and see a smile, or in Joel's case, a frown, come by. For the rest of the day, the phones kept ringing. Finally, during lunch, I put the phones on the message machine and called Mr. Robbins back. He sounded like a pleasant man. He was extremely nice. He asked if I had chosen the apartment that I wanted and he wondered when I wanted to move in. Sure, I had chosen one, the second one, and I told him where it was located.

"I would like to move in one month, if that's fine with you."

"That'll be fine, but you can move in tomorrow if you want to."

"Well, thanks, but I need to give my landlord some notice."

"Okay, if that's what you want."

I thought not really, but it was the right thing to do. Mr. Robbins told me to come down to his office on Saturday and fill out the paperwork. I got a little frightened hearing that.

"It's just a legality, but don't worry about anything; you're all set."

"Thank you."

I hung up the phone. A new place without bugs, drugs, or thugs. I was too thrilled! I called Robert's voice mail to thank him for everything and to invite him to dinner. I transferred the calls back to me, then checked the voice messages. Patrick had called to say that he couldn't make his meeting today. I figured Karan would be disappointed hearing that. Then I transferred his call to Kyle. Some of the guys came in and some left. I finally got a call from Robert, congratulating me on the new apartment and accepting my dinner invitation. By the end of the day, I was exhausted. I wished I had not made plans with Robert. The phone rang all day, and then some of the appointments were mixed up that Karan had arranged. I didn't know what she had been thinking about lately, but her business sense was going to heck. I had to clean up some pretty big mistakes she had been making lately.

Robert came back right before I got off. He asked me to wait on him and that he would be out in a moment. He stayed in his office for about 15 minutes before coming out, then we got on the elevator. The elevator stopped on the sixth floor. My heart stopped beating. I kept praying, *God, pleassse don't let her get on; please don't let her get on.* She got on. She looked at me. Then she looked at Robert.

She said, "Hey, it's Nikki, right?"

"Yeah, how are you doing, Niyokia?"

"Fine, and you?"

"Fine."

I knew that my tone was dry, and I think that she knew it too. She hit the third floor. I knew it was all over by now. We went on down to the parking garage. I had been quiet, and when we got into the car, Robert said, "You're worried by what she's going to say, aren't you?"

"No, but you should be."

He drove us to the same hotel that I had gone to lunch with Kyle when I first started working at the firm.

"Mr. Jackson, are you trying to tell me something?"

With a very puzzled look on his face he said, "No, this is just one of my favorite places to eat."

"Yeah, it is nice."

He looked at me and said, "Oh, you've been here before?"

I thought, *Oh, oh, I just opened my mouth toooo much.* I looked straight ahead and said "Yeah, Kyle brought me here once for lunch."

"Oh, I see."

We went in. After we were seated at our table and our drinks were brought, Robert finally said, "I don't want you to take this the wrong way, but you need to be careful about Kyle."

I was really thinking that he sounded jealous.

"He's a good lawyer, but he's also a womanizer, and I don't want to see you get hurt."

"I'm not interested in Kyle."

He didn't flinch when I said that he just said okay. We ordered our meal. I had some kind of chicken pasta thing. We talked and laughed, and I made sure that I kept my drinking to a minimum. Robert told me about some of his college days and although I laughed at many of his jokes, I noticed that he had a very dry sense of humor. After dinner, he took me home. He wanted to come up, but I thought that it wouldn't be a good idea for him to leave his car out front. He said okay. I was getting ready to get out the car when he touched my hand. I turned towards him, and he looked at me so tenderly I leaned over and he leaned over and our mouths touched so very carefully. It wasn't like the kiss we had yesterday. It was different, softer and sweeter. I smiled as I leaned back and said that I would see him tomorrow.

"Well, actually, I have some work to do out of town, so I won't be back until Friday night," he said.

"What am I supposed to do 'til then?"

"Can I call you?"

"I hope that you will."

Then I turned and got out of the car. As I walked into the apartment building, I felt as if I was floating, and on top of that, I would be leaving this hellhole soon. Things couldn't get any better.

The next day I wasn't in any hurry to get to work because I knew that Robert would not be there, but still I made it on time. I went through my usual routine but with a lack of enthusiasm. I thought things would not be the same around here without him, and just when I thought there would be no drama, the drama mama came to work. She rushed over to my desk.

"So, Robert is back to taking you home, I see."

"Yes, he is." This time, I said it with a smile.

"Oh, I see." Then she lowered her eyes with a smirk on her face and said, "So, is there anything I should know about?"

"No."

"Oh, I see. You don't want to tell anyone yet. That's fine, I can wait."

"You can say what you want to; it isn't going to change the truth."

"Hey, I wasn't meaning anything about it; I know that he just takes you home sometimes. I was just hoping, you know, for his sake and yours, that some sparks might fly. You know that he has been alone for quite some time."

"Really?"

"Yes, he needs someone, and I was hoping that you could possibly fill that void in his life."

"Really? But not too long ago, you were saying that I should stay in my place, remember?"

"Oh, that, well, I just didn't want you to get hurt."

"And now, it's okay for me to get hurt?"

"You're just twisting everything." With some attitude, Karan went into her office. I laughed and scratched my head as she closed the door. *Okay, bring it on.*

Then the elevator doors opened and out stepped a man. He was dressed in casual clothes, and he carried some flowers.

"My I help you?"

"Yes, I have a delivery."

I took the flowers and read the card to see who they were for. The card said, "These are for you until I get back~Robert." I thanked the deliveryman and put the note in my purse. I did not want to give Karan or anyone else any ammunition. But the biggest smile crept across my face as I looked at the flowers that took up *whole* table behind my desk. Robert was so kind. The mail came and, boy, it was a lot, but it did not faze me, even though I wasn't able to sort it right away. The phones were ringing, and the guys were coming in asking questions. Then Joel came out of his office and stood right in front of my desk, asking,

"Has the mail come yet?"

"Yes, but it isn't sorted."

He looked over at my flowers and said, "I'm looking for something very important. When you find time to do your job, I would appreciate it if you don't get it mixed up this time."

Normally, that would bother me, but not today. No, today I received flowers from someone who really cared about me and *nothing* was going to mess up my day—especially Joel. I just smiled at him. For some reason, that seemed to anger him. He started to walk away, then turned abruptly and said,

"Shouldn't you deliver those to whoever they belong to?"

I shook it off and started sorting the mail. I was *not* going to give him the pleasure. I got his pile all ready and immediately took it to him. I didn't really give him a chance to say come in after I knocked on the door either. I just put the mail in its appropriate spot and left. I went back to my desk to finish some other tasks. The phone began vying for

Illegal Love | 73

my attention; it was Buffy asking for George. I transferred her call. It came back to me.

"I got his voice mail."

"Then that must mean he isn't here."

"Well, when do you expect to hear from him?"

"I don't know. He hasn't called in today."

"Will you tell him I called, please?"

I took the phone off my ear and looked at it. Then I put it back and said, "Okay, Buffy, I will." She had never uttered those words to me before. That was probably the first time she had ever said please to anyone. He must have had that talk with her. Shortly after that, George came in, so I told him that she had called. He told me to patch her through the next time. *Okay, you made up.* I knew it wouldn't last for long.

At some time during the day, Patrick came by. He didn't really say anything to me, but he looked like he was trying to creep past Karan's office. He and Kyle left the building together. On several occasions, Karan came out, but I didn't tell her that he had already been here. She finally noticed my flowers.

"Oh, my, we have an admirer?"

"Yes, I do."

"Who are they from?"

"A new friend."

"And what is his name?"

"Names are not important."

I didn't want to lie, but it really wasn't any of her business. She shrugged her shoulders and went back to her office, probably realizing that I was not going to tell her what she wanted to know.

Last night, I had written a letter to my apartment complex manager, letting him know I would not be keeping my place much longer. Today I called to see if he had gotten it. The girl that answered the phone said they had and that they would be sorry to see me leave. I was one of the few tenants that paid rent on time. I thanked her. It was nice to know that someone paid attention to the things that I was trying to do right in my life. I went to take the mail around to the others, but I felt hollow when I got to Robert's office. I missed him already. I wondered why. When I got to my desk, there were three calls, back to back. The first one was Buffy calling for George again.

"Is he in?"

"Yes, just a moment, please."

"Thank you."

I patched her through.

The second call was Robert for me.

"How are you?"

"Fine, and how are you?"

"Not too good."

"What's wrong?"

He said, "Well, I miss a certain someone."

I smiled and said, "She's missing you too."

The other line rang, so I put him on hold. This call was for Karan. I patched it through, then went back to talking to Robert.

"Thank you for the roses."

"No problem. I wanted you to have something from me to look at all week, even if you couldn't see me."

"That's so wonderful of you, and it will work, too. Every time I see them, I'll think of you."

Just then, I heard something crash in Karan's office. I told Robert to hold on again, but he said that he had to go and that he would call me tonight when he got to his room. He said he was sorry that he wouldn't be here to take me home. I told him it was fine, I was used to the bus.

Hanging up quickly, I ran to Karan's office to see if she was all right. She had thrown something made out of glass at the door. Shards of glass were all over the floor by the time I got there, and she was standing there looking hurt and damaged.

"I'll clean this up."

"Leave it. I'll get it later."

I walked out of her office concerned about her. But since she didn't want any help, I put the phones on the message machine and went downstairs to the cafeteria for lunch. Since Robert wasn't in, I decided to eat down there. I found a private little place in a corner. There was a short wall in between me and the other table with plants on top of it. I thought I heard Niyokia's voice and some other women speaking, so I just peeked through the fake flowers a little and yes, it was her. I could even hear some of what she was saying.

One girl said, "Well, are they seeing each other or not?"

Niyokia said, "I personally don't see *what* he would see in her, but they are always together. Karan says that she keeps denying any involvement with him."

Then another woman said, "Well, I tell you, I even tried, and he wasn't budging."

Someone else said, "Oh, I didn't know that you had tried."

She replied, "Yeah, girl, one day I got a flat tire, and you know how kind he is. He got out and fixed it."

She continued, "I even had on a low-cut blouse. I leaned over him while he was fixing the tire, and you know, most men can't resist these two sisters.

"But you know what he did? *Nothing.* Not even an agreeable smile. Then I tried to invite him to dinner, you know, to thank him, and he said that it not necessary, that he was just doing his duty as a man to help out a beautiful woman in distress."

One of the women retorted, "Yeah, beautiful—my ass!"

The woman that was talking before said, "And what is *that* supposed to mean? I look just as good as you do."

Niyokia said, "Why don't you both just shut up. I have some new news."

They all got quiet. I even stopped chewing on my salad.

She said, "You know the big law firm on the 20th floor is hiring a new paralegal."

In harmony, they all said, "Uh-huh."

She said, "Well, guess who *didn't* get the job?"

One of the women replied, "No ..."

Niyokia said, "Yeah, and she was just positive she had it in the bag. She had even started spending her new salary already."

Someone asked, "What do you mean?"

"Well, she went out and bought a new car with some money she had been saving for some big bill that she had."

Someone snickered. "You *got* to be kidding me. How do you spend money before you know that you have money coming in to replace it?"

Niyokia said, "Well, she thought that she had the most wonderful interview with them, and since they were all in the same building, she thinks that she had friends up there. She should be getting her phone call today."

One girl said, "I saw her drive in today. She wasn't in a new car."

"She had them order it. Custom this and custom that."

They all laughed. They were talking about Karan. I looked at the time. It was time for me to leave, and I didn't want them to see me, so

I sneaked around the other way and went back upstairs. I felt bad for Karan. Not only did she not get the job she was trying to get, but also she didn't realize that these women that she thought were her friends weren't. I felt really sad for her. When I got back to the office, her door was still shut. I wanted to go talk with her, but felt it was not any of my business. After a while, she came out of her office.

One of our clients came in. She got angry and started getting loud because Karan had messed up her appointment, and George was not available to take her. She had been given a wrong appointment date. Karan had been apologizing and trying to calm the woman down when Kyle came in with Patrick. Karan, who was not in a great mood, was not being successful in getting the woman under control. Kyle said that he would see her and that he would talk with Karan later. Then he told Patrick that he would call him later.

Patrick looked like he was trying to make a clean get away when Karan called him. He turned around, like he really didn't want to. He had this fake smile plastered on his face as he said, "Hey, what's up? Where you been? I've been trying to get in contact with you."

She moved closer to him so that I would not be able to hear their conversation. I saw him make some hand gestures, then he said, "Well, we'll talk about it later."

I saw the different facial expressions he went through, and none of them looked good.

"Okay, I'll wait until you call me later on," Karan said, none too happy.

That was loud enough for me to hear. Then she walked away and came to my desk as he got on the elevator.

"Oh, so you and Patrick are kicking it now," I remarked.

She smiled and said, "Well, we're trying to do a little something-something."

I smiled at her and said, "That's good. You need to be happy too."

She started to walk away, but turned and looked at me, and said, "Does this new guy make you happy?"

"Yes, but it's nothing but a friendship right now."

As she walked into her office, Kyle came out of his office with the irate lady from earlier. When she walked past Karan's door, she didn't even look her way. Kyle knocked on her door and went in. He stayed in there for a little while. I guessed they were talking about what had happened. When he came out, he said to me, "Karan will talk with you in a little while."

I got nervous. Was I about to be fired? Did she lie about me? I didn't make appointments. What now? Here it goes: *Sorry but we are having some cutbacks and things are not working the way that we intended them to.* Karan called me on the phone, which she never did. I went into her office. When I got in there, I automatically sat down.

She said, "You're not going to be in here long."

I *really* thought this was it then.

"Kyle, well, Kyle and I feel that I might have too much on my hands right now with running everything, so we're going to give you some more duties, if you don't mind."

"Sure. Whatever."

In my mind, I thought, *as long as I have a job.* She said, "Starting Monday, you'll be making all the appointments, and then I will gradually train you on some of the other stuff I do around here, just in case I need some backup. Is that okay with you?"

"Yeah."

Then she said, "You can leave now."

I got up and walked out. I was relieved. That was all I felt. Periodically, she would come over and ask me to move from my desk so that she could do something on my computer, and then leave. She wouldn't bother to tell me what she was doing. By the end of the day, I still didn't know what she had done. I finally left the office feeling bad because Robert wasn't home. Then Kyle caught the elevator with me and asked if I wanted to go out for drinks after work. I told him that I was waiting on a very special call so I had to hurry home.

"Okay, maybe tomorrow then."

He was persistent, I must give him that. When I got home, Robert had not called, and I was glad. I did my evening ritual of washing my face, brushing my teeth, and cuddling up with a good book. The one I was reading now was *THIS CRAZY LIFE OF MINE,* by Felicia Truttier. I was really into it when the phone rang.

"Hello."

"Hello, Nikki."

My smile could have lit up my apartment.

"Hello, traveler."

"How is everything at work?"

I told him about everything that had happened.

"I'm going to start packing this weekend. I should be able to move 2 weeks after that."

"Well, you can count me in for the big move, and I'll see who else I can get to help."

"Thanks."

We continued to talk for another half hour before he said, "I'll let you go to sleep now and will talk with you tomorrow."

"I miss you."

"Good. I miss you too."

Somehow, from that, I felt like we were on the verge of something.

Friday finally came, and the office was doing its usual buzz. Karan had put all the associates' schedule on my computer and had been showing me how to set up the appointments during the week. It didn't seem so hard except she said that sometimes they would change things and that it was up to me to effect that change. Other appointments would have to coincide with those new changes. I felt since I didn't do a lot at the front desk, this would not be so hard. Karan didn't have a bad attitude about it, and said that she would still keep her planner updated, so that meant that she would check on me every day to do her updating. I didn't have a problem with that.

The phones kept ringing off the hook all day, and it was a little hard checking to see who was calling for an appointment and who was calling to speak with an associate for consultations. I knew that somehow, though, I would eventually get it right. Morning mail came and I sorted it and delivered it to everyone. Many of the guys were not in the office right now because they had court, and the most wonderful thing about that was Joel was one of them. I went to lunch down in the cafeteria again today, of course, hoping that I would see or hear Niyokia and her friends talking, but they were not there. When I went to sit down, I noticed Tom.

"May I sit down and have lunch with you?" I asked.

"Sur—re."

We had lunch together. He didn't talk much during lunch; every now and then he would ask me something about how work was going. He wanted me to know that he was pleased to have me on board. I finished my meal before him, then went back upstairs. Several calls had come in, and Kyle had left some instructions of things he wanted me to do while he was out. When I looked at the list, I was shocked because

Illegal Love | 79

I didn't know what to do. I went to Karan and asked her. She looked at the list, and her eyes showed that she was not happy.

"Oh, well, we talked, and he wants you to be more like my backup person, so I guess I have to show you how to do these things."

"Okay, I'm ready when you are."

"It won't be today."

"But Kyle wants these things done today."

"I'll do them."

"Okay."

I walked out of the office, and Karan was on the phone before I hit the door. My day consisted of taking messages, sorting mail, and filing my nails for the 200th time. By the end of the day, I was ready to go because I knew that Robert would be home soon and that tomorrow, I would go to talk with Mr. Robbins about my new apartment. I was shutting down my computer for the day when I got a phone call. It was Robert.

"How are you doing?"

"Wonderful, now."

"That's good."

"You caught me just in time; I was getting ready to leave."

"I know. That's why I called."

"Oh, yeah?"

"Yeah."

"Do you want a ride home?"

"Are you downstairs?"

"Yes."

"I'm on my way."

I almost ran to the elevator. On the way down, I realized in my hurry that I had forgotten to transfer the calls to the message machine. I stopped the elevator and went back up. When I got into the office, I heard two people talking. It sounded like Karan and Joel. I tried to be quiet and went to my desk to transfer the phone calls. As I was leaving, I distinctively heard Karan say, "No, she actually is working out *too* well. Kyle wants her to be my backup, and you know what that means. If he wants to, he'll be able to get rid of me—and maybe you, too, later on."

Joel said, "Well, I'll see what I can do about it."

She said, "Good, this is getting ridiculous. Kyle is forgetting who was here with him when he started and had nothing, and who helped him get started in the first place."

I tiptoed out of the office. I didn't feel so wonderful now. I went down and got into the car. Robert said, "I had hoped that you would be happier to see me."

"I am, it's ... I just got some bad news."

"Well, don't worry about it. I'll make it better. How would you like to spend the weekend at my place?"

I looked over at him, and he quickly added, "No, not like that. It'll be totally innocent. It's just that I have some briefs to work on, and I thought that if you were there helping me, I could get through them more quickly."

"Sure, just take me by the house to pick up some things."

"You know I still have the sleep attire you wore last time."

I smiled and said, "Yeah, but I'd rather have my own."

We went to my place to get some of my things. I invited him up with me. He parked the car, and we walked into my building. I was still a little embarrassed because his apartment was so clean. Just coming up the stairs, you could see the graffiti on the walls and smell the urine. Not to mention the people under me had an old beat-up reclining chair sitting in the hall that sometimes you would see people sleeping on. I was just lucky today the usual crowd was not here, sitting out playing cards or drinking; sometimes they would even be smoking marijuana. Robert didn't seem to be turned off by the scene, but I knew it was more than he expected.

We went into my apartment. I was glad that I had cleaned up this week. He had a seat on my old beat-up sofa that did not match my chair. Robert was so kind; he said that it was very soft. I got a few things, and we were off. Next, we stopped by a Chinese restaurant and got some take-out. It was nice he knew the owner, and they talked and pointed at me and laughed. When we got back to the car, I asked him what they talked about. He told me that the man's name was Wong, and Wong wanted to know who you were since he had not seen me with a woman for a very long time. I told him that you were the mother of my children. Then he said that he didn't know that I had any children, and I said, not yet.

Illegal Love | 81

I smiled all the way back to his apartment. When we got to his place, it was only the second time I had been here, but it still looked so beautiful.

"We'll eat first and then start working," he suggested.

We had fun eating, and we even ate in the living room. We just talked and talked. Robert was eloquent in everything he said. He had such a way with words. I thought he must never lose a case. Men and women alike would be mesmerized by his speech. I wondered how he could like someone like me. I'm sure I was not the kind of person he was used to dating. But then, we weren't actually dating either. When we finished, we cleaned up the area and went to work. Robert was right; there were a lot of things to go through. He showed me what he needed me to do and put me at the dining room table to do it. Then he went into the living room to do his part. After a few hours, my eyes began getting tired from all the reading I was doing. Of course, I didn't understand any of it, but all I had to do was to highlight certain things.

Time flew by and then he came over and said, "Okay, time for bed."

"I'm not tired."

"Yeah, but I don't want you to wear yourself out on the first night."

"Oh, okay."

I stopped what I was doing and went into the bedroom to get ready for bed. Then I thought about something and called him. He stuck his head into the room.

"Are you taking me to Mr. Robbins' tomorrow?"

"Yes, I had planned on it."

"Thank you."

I went into the bathroom for my shower. It looked smaller somehow but I guess it was because I was standing up this time and not sitting on the floor, looking up. Your perspective made all the difference. I opened the shower door and turned on the water, then sat on the toilet while I waited for it to get to the right temperature. By the time I stepped into the shower, I realized that I did not have a washcloth or towel, so I called my knight in shining armor again.

"Robert!"

At first I thought he didn't hear me, but suddenly there he was, standing in the doorway.

"Yes, ma'am."

"I forgot to get a towel."

"Hold on."

"A washcloth, too."

He came to the shower with his head turned so he could not see my nakedness. When he opened the door and handed me the washcloth, I grabbed his arm and pulled him in.

"What are you doing?"

"Having some fun."

I kissed him, and he kissed me back. The water splashed over our bodies and soaked his clothes. When we stopped kissing, I couldn't take my eyes off of him. I pulled his shirt out of his pants and pulled it over his head. He let me, not helping, but not withdrawing either. Next, I unbuttoned his pants and pulled them down. He had to help me by stepping out of them. I smiled as he did this. I threw his things out of the shower. By now, thoroughly aroused, I leaned my wet body onto his and hugged him, and he hugged me back. I could feel his hardness pressed up against me. I looked into his eyes hungry and started kissing him. The water felt wonderful. It acted like an aphrodisiac and stimulated my nerve endings, adding to the pleasure I was about to receive.

Robert grabbed my hair and held my head back. Then he started kissing my neck, biting me gently and sucking me passionately. His teeth went down to my breast and he gently ran them over my nipples, which became erect with his touch. Then he went back up to my mouth. His body was hot, but mine was hotter. I turned around and rubbed my ass over his now-protruding lovemaking machine and felt it harden with every motion. We moved together. He sank his teeth into my flesh. I moaned for him. We were just getting ready to make love when the water suddenly turned cold. It must have been getting cold for a while, but we were so into each other we didn't notice.

He said, "Can we continue this outside?"

I turned off the water and opened the door. Picking up a towel, I dried every part of his body, giving particular attention to those areas that seemed to be calling to me. Then Robert took the towel out of my hands and gently rubbed me dry, spending extra time at the source of my heat. I couldn't take it any longer and pulled him into the bedroom. He lay me down gently on the bed, then stood over me, softly kissing every inch of me from the top of my body down to my ankles, and then up again. His soft, sweet lips sent shivers throughout my body. I wanted him, but I was trying to be patient. He surprised me by sitting on the floor and putting one of my feet on his chest as he held the other in his hands and massaged it ever so gently. This was a new experience for me. It felt wonderful and made me relax. No one had ever given me a foot massage before. No one had ever taken the time to see what I wanted before.

Then Robert massaged the other foot. When he finished, he kissed my body all the way back up again. Finally, he lay on top of me as I opened myself for him. He inserted himself inside of me and as I had hoped, it was a perfect fit. I couldn't have imagined it feeling so good. We moved together with a rhythm as if we had been making love with each other forever. His moves were mine, and mine his. Up and down, in and out, slow, like the moving of two lovers never wanting to part. My ending was his beginning, and we were never going to be separated again. My nails dug deep into his flesh as I felt his manhood rising to the point of explosion and as he did, so did I. We collapsed, he on top of me, and me with my legs wrapped around him. After a while, he slid off the bed and went to shower. I wasn't sure if the water was hot again, but I ran into the bathroom and got into the shower with him. It was a little warm by then, but we quickly bathed and got out and got ready for bed. Like a true gent, he asked if it was okay if he stayed in the master bedroom with me.

"Yes, I don't have anything to hide from you."

But in truth, I knew that I did. I just hoped that he hadn't noticed yet. We got into bed. I lay on my side, and he lay on his side facing me. We slept contentedly 'til morning.

When morning came, I woke up alone. I didn't even remember him leaving the bed, but he must have heard me stirring.

"Good morning, sleepyhead."

I sat up in the bed, and my lover came into the room.

"I wasn't sure if you were going to get up anytime soon, but I didn't want to wake you."

"This bed is so soft I just couldn't seem to get out of it. But I'm up now, and we should be starting our day."

"I was just waiting on you."

I jumped out of the bed and went into the bathroom. I could see Robert making up the bed. I brushed my teeth, my hair, and went to find my clothes. He had them neatly laid out on a chair in the bay window of his bedroom. I thought I could never live with this man. I dressed, and we got ready to go to breakfast.

He said, "Do you want to drive?"

"No, if anything happened to your car while I was driving, I'd never forgive myself."

Robert drove to the local Breakfast Spot. As we ate, we talked about the work he wanted to continue when we got back to his place. I wanted to talk about us, or at least last night, or if there would be an us. Instead, I just listened as he went on about a case that was coming up. He was very passionate about his work; he truly believed in what he was doing and gave his all to it.

We left The Breakfast Spot and headed towards what I assumed was the office where we would meet Mr. Robbins. When we got there, we met a tall, attractive white male in his mid-40s with sandy-brown hair who was about 5'11. He probably didn't weigh more than 165 lbs, and he had the cutest little gray patch of hair in the front of his hairline. I don't know why, I just assumed that he would be black, but I guess it didn't matter. He was very nice, and he always called me Ms. Nikki. We went over the agreement with him. He explained everything to me before I sighed anything, and then he asked me if I understood everything. I looked at Robert to see if he had any questions, but he didn't.

"Yes."

Although I signed a year's lease, he said that our agreement would be for as long as I desired to stay in the apartment, and the rent would never change. I agreed and signed every spot marked with an x. Then he handed me my keys.

"Welcome to Cherry Blossom Hills."

Robert looked at me. "I thought you loved the Granite Place apartment."

"I love them all, but I especially love the one that's closest to you."

He smiled and held my hand. We left Mr. Robbins and went by my new apartment. It was wonderful saying, "my apartment." It was beautiful. I wondered how my not-so-beautiful furniture would fit into this place. Robert said, "Don't worry; I'll have it looking beautiful by the time you move in." I asked him if he wanted to christen the apartment right now.

"Here on this floor? Nikki, I don't know about you, but being bare-assed on a floor that I'm not sure who walked on it last, well, that's not exciting to me. We'll have plenty of time to do that when you move in."

"Plenty?"

"Yes, unless there's something you want to tell me."

"No."

I was happy for that remark, and I drew myself closer to him as we walked out. Then we went straight back to his apartment, which was not too far, only a block or two.

Robert set out his papers again, and we started working, and soon I was bored. But I knew that I had come not only to be close to Robert, but I also wanted to help him and see if I could learn anything from this experience. I also wanted to get up the nerve to tell him what I had overheard Friday, but so far, all we had done was work. So I just plunged into what I was doing for the next couple of hours. He finally came in to see if everything was going okay, and I showed him all the things I had done. He took them back over to the living room, then returned.

"Break time."

I slumped on the table and said, "Finally!"

"Okay, what do you want?"

I told him that I didn't care, as long as it was outside. I grabbed my purse, and we went to get something at a little spot down the street. It was such a nice day that we decided to walk instead of drive. The Old Kitchen Café is where we ended up. It was cute. On the outside, it looked like an old, run-down café, but on the inside, it was really nice and modern. We ordered and talked. I asked him how well he knew Karan and Joel.

"Well, I know they have been with Kyle ever since he got started. I guess Kyle keeps Joel on because of that.

"Joel could be a good lawyer, but he has a bad attitude, and he doesn't care about his clients or what their needs are. He wins some, and he loses a lot, and he doesn't care one way or the other."

I shook my head and said, "And Karan?"

"Karan is Joel's sister, and that could be the reason she's still there."

"His *sister*—but they don't look alike, act alike, or even have the same last name."

"Oh, they act similar. She is sneaky in a different kind of way. She's like a black widow spider. All she's interested in is seeing how many people she can trap in her web before she devours them. At least with

Joel, you'll know if he doesn't like you up front, but with Karan, she will slowly stab you in the back."

I thought how that made so much sense.

"What about their last names?"

"Oh, they were separated by adoption. Some years after they were adults, they found each other. I think they even live in the same neighborhood. They are hardly ever far away from each other."

I had been trying to trust her and confide in her and all that time, she was planning my execution. Now I told Robert what I had overheard and he said, "I'll talk with Kyle, and you should watch your back."

"I'll make sure that I'm really careful from now on."

Then he brought up last night.

"You shocked me yesterday."

I raised an eyebrow. "Really? How?"

"Don't act shy. I know that wasn't your style."

"Well, I kinda got tired of waiting on you."

"Waiting on *me*? How do you know that's what I wanted?"

"You don't expect me to believe that you just wanted me to come over for the weekend to work."

He looked at me with a straight face. "Yes, I did."

"Well, I'm sorry that I spoiled your plans."

He was about to say something, but I flicked some water at him. We started laughing and got ready to leave. On the way back to the apartment, we held hands and I leaned on his shoulder. I was happy, no matter what else was going on. I was happy this moment. We went back to work. Later that night as we were making love, I thought that it was better than it had been the day before. Maybe it was because we both had gotten over being sorta nervous. Robert was so gentle and tender. I could tell that he wanted to please my every desire. When sleep finally came, it was welcome; after all, we had been at it most of the night.

Sunday morning arrived, and Robert wanted me to get up and go to church with him. He should have told me before now, because I didn't come prepared. I told him he could take me home if he wanted, but he said no that I could stay until he got back, so I continued working. When he got back, we went to lunch. He looked *so* handsome. I was used to seeing him in suits, but today, he looked especially handsome. After lunch, we went back to finish our work. By then, he had changed into some shorts and a T-shirt, but even in his casualness, he was neat and handsome. Today it seemed that we got less work done. He was actually in a playful mood. We wrestled and kissed and then, of course, we made love right in the breezeway between the living room and the dining room.

After exhausting ourselves in each other, we lay there in our God-given bodies au naturel just resting. I watched him sleep a while. He breathed just a little hard, but never making any real sounds. I watched his eyes dart back and forth and wondered what he was dreaming about. I hoped it was me. When he awoke, we showered, and then I got ready to go home.

He told me that the next time I come over, I should bring more stuff so that I can just leave from here for work. I said I would. When I got home, I was in heaven. I couldn't wait until he called me. I got my clothes ready for work and waited. I almost fell asleep waiting though because when he called, it was late.

He said, "I came home to get caught up on the work that we didn't finish today."

"I'm sorry; I should have stayed a little later."

"It's okay. You can make it up to me later. I'll come and pick you up in the morning for work around 8:00."

"Yes, sir."

Then we said good night to each other, and I rolled over on my bed, but I could hardly sleep from the joy I was feeling inside. But what should have been another wonderful night of sleep ended up being a terrible nightmare. In my dream, a monster was chasing me. Robert was on the other side of this river, and I kept trying to make my way to him so that he could save me, but the closer I got to Robert, the closer a monster got to me. I woke up screaming and sweating. I grabbed one of the teddy bears I had on the bed next to me for comfort. I wanted to forget it, but I knew who the monster was and he was not that far away anymore. For the rest of the night, I slept with the lights on, but sleep still did not come right away.

Monday morning I was quick to get up. I didn't want Robert to have to come up to get me. He called when he got downstairs, and I ran out the door. I got into the car, kissed him, he said, "Good morning, honey," smiled, and off we drove. When we got to work, no one else was there, so we gave each other a kiss before he went to his office. I did my usual with the coffee and then the messages. I went through them to see who needed appointments and the rest I transferred to the appropriate associate. Finally, everyone else started coming in and I greeted each one of them with a joyful smile.

Karan looked at me and said, "What got into you this morning?"

"I'm always happy, but today, I am just happier!"

"You must have gotten some this weekend, huh?"

I didn't answer her, but I didn't say no either. She smiled as she went to her office, occasionally looking back at me with her deceitful smirk. Even when Joel came through the office, I was on my best behavior.

"Good morning, Joel."

He looked at me.

"Morning."

I went and got everyone's coffee and took it around. After that, I went to get Robert's hot chocolate. I knocked on the door and went in. He was standing by the window with his jacket off. I wanted him right then and there. Quickly I closed the door and brought it over to his desk.

"Thank you."

I waited. I wanted to kiss him, but he didn't make any moves to come over to where I was, so I moved closer to him.

"Hey, stranger, are you going to come over here or what?"

He turned to look at me. "Nikki, we're at work."

That stopped me in my tracks.

"Oh, I'm sorry."

I turned to go out of the door, and he came over and grabbed me by the waist.

"What's going on with you?"

"If you wanted to keep us a secret, you should have just let me know and I could have caught the bus this morning."

"It isn't that, I just think there are places for everything, and well, work is for work."

"I don't really work like that. If we are together, then we are together—at work and at play, and if not—then we are not."

He held on to me, then he turned me around and kissed me gently.

"How is that? Is that reassurance enough that we are together?"

I kissed him back.

"Yes, for now."

I walked out of the office and to my surprise, Karan was there, standing at my desk.

Illegal Love | 89

"You sure have been in there a long time."

"I wasted his chocolate and had to clean it up."

"Just be careful. They have some sensitive documents around here."

"I know. What was it that you wanted to talk with me about?"

"Nothing really. I was just checking to see if Patrick had called. Maybe I was out or something."

"No, not to my knowledge."

She looked off in a distance then said, "Oh, I just thought maybe I had missed his call. We were supposed to be doing something together tonight. Oh, well ..."

"I promise when he does call, I'll let you know."

She went to her office, and I went to my desk, awaiting my daily mail. I really just wanted another excuse to go back into Robert's office. The mail came, and I sorted it. I was getting ready to deliver it when Robert came out of his office.

"Just put it on my desk. I have a meeting, but I'll be back in time to pick you up this afternoon."

This time, he did not look around. He just leaned over and kissed me on the lips. But I turned to see if anyone was around; no one was. I wasn't sure if I was glad or mad. I delivered the mail. By the end of the day, I was ready to see my baby. I went downstairs, and he was there at the front, waiting for me. I didn't care if anyone saw us, but I did look around anyway. He drove towards my house.

"Are you staying over at my house tonight, or are you going home?" he asked.

"Is that an invitation?"

He looked over with his best puppy-dog look.

"Must I beg?"

"No, that was enough."

We stopped by my house so I could pick up some things. This continued for the next 8 months. On and off from my new place to his, we were together all the time. And, of course, by now Karan, Niyokia, and the whole building knew that we were together.

Chapter 7

Every morning except on the mornings that he had to go to a meeting, Robert would come by the apartment and pick me up if I wasn't at his place or he wasn't at mine. One morning when he dropped me off, I went upstairs to find Karan at my desk. I didn't say anything except good morning, but I could tell that I had startled her. She had not even turned the lights on.

"Oh, I wasn't expecting you so early," she said hastily.

"Robert had an early meeting, and he wanted to make sure that I got to work on time."

"That was sweet of him."

"That's why I like him so."

She looked at me like billy goat gruff.

"If you're finished, I need to sit at my desk and get set up for the day," I said.

By now, I was not only doing the appointments, but I was doing some of the typing and proofing some of documents for most of the lawyers. Of course, Joel still insisted that Karan do all of his work, and I didn't argue about it. Patrick's case had been won, and we were working on another problem regarding him. It was an assault case with the girl that was his alibi from the last case. He claimed he didn't touch her, but she claimed that he had roughed her up to get her to testify for him. It was more money for the firm. Patrick's and Karan's little fling didn't last long. Shortly after the case was won, he didn't come back to us until he needed us again, but he never went back to Karan. In fact, her disgust for him had really increased more than before.

I wasn't making coffee anymore, but I was checking the message machine to make sure there weren't any appointments. After seeing that there weren't any, I transferred the calls. Robert called after the mail had come and said he wanted to try and meet me for lunch. I told him that would be fine. Kyle brought me a couple of things to work on for the day, and the phones were going at it. I had made sure that everything was up-to-date before I left for lunch. I didn't want any problems. I had made it this far knowing that Karan and Joel didn't want me there, and I wasn't about to let my guard down.

Robert was downstairs waiting for me. I kissed him when I got into the car. He drove off. I kept trying to see where we were going. We usually went to one of the restaurants near the office unless something big happened, like he won a case or something, but as far as I knew, there weren't any cases at this time.

"Hun, where're we going?" I said in my best country-girl tone.

"You just *had* to ask, didn't you? You just will *not* let me give you a surprise."

"Oh, one of those again," I said in a bland voice. I was playing and luckily, he knew it.

"Okay, I'll be a good girl and wait."

I smiled at him and turned around in my seat like an innocent little girl. "Do you want me to close my eyes, too?"

"Only if you want to. This is your surprise."

We drove for a little while longer, and then we parked in the yard of someone who had a very nice older model BMW sitting there. I thought this was a weird place to go to lunch. It better be good 'cause I was getting pretty hungry. Robert honked his horn, and an old lady came out. She was really old, with white hair and a cane. She wore a long housedress that looked to be almost longer than she was. The glasses she wore had fallen down to her nose, and with every step she took, they looked as if they would fall off. Robert got out of the car.

"Good afternoon, Mrs. Taylor."

"Mr. Jackson, is that you again?"

"Yes, ma'am, it's me again."

"Baby, how many times you gonna come around?"

"Well, hopefully, this will be the last time."

"I have the keys ready for you and all the paperwork. My son John put them in the car."

I was still sitting in the car until Robert asked me to come and look at the older BMW that was in the yard. It was a nice car and looked practically new. I could tell that she had taken good care of it. It really looked in wonderful condition.

As I was looking into the window, Robert came over, unlocked the door, and opened it up. He asked me to sit in it and tell me what I thought. I thought my baby was buying another car but why an old one? But I got into it. The interior was immaculate, the floors looked like they had never been stepped on, and I loved it.

"Robert, if you are planning on buying it, it looks great in my eyes."

"Crank it up."

It purred.

"Whoever had this car loved it, and it shows."

"Yes, my husband, Mr. Taylor, loved this car, and I just couldn't drive it after he passed, but I kept it up though, taking it down to Joe's every other month to make sure it was working fine. Now John, my son, says it's time to sell it. I just hope that you love it as much as Mr. Taylor did."

Robert turned to the old lady and said, "Oh, she will."

I looked up from the driver's seat. "Robert, you didn't buy me this car, did you?"

"Yes, I did."

He leaned in the car and said, "Don't be mad. I just thought that it was time you had your own transportation instead of waiting on me or the bus."

"I was going to buy a car just as soon as I got my raise."

"Well, just think of it like this: when you get your raise, you can buy new furniture. The car really didn't cost as much as you think, and I'll make sure that you pay me back if you want to. We can start on it tonight."

I leaned forward and kissed him. This man of mine's only thought was to please me. I wanted to cry, but I knew he wouldn't understand. He told her that we were going to take it with us, took out his checkbook, and wrote her a check for $2,000.

"We'll take it home and sometime this week, we'll have all the paperwork changed over to your name."

I was on cloud nine as I drove the car. Everything seemed so wonderful. I could not believe that I had a car, a job, a nice apartment, and a man that really loved me. We took the car to my apartment and for the first time, I got to park in my assigned parking space. Life couldn't get much better than this.

We got back to the office late, and my new moment of happiness was about to be put on hold. Things were all screwed up. Kyle, Joel, and Karan were at my desk. I don't know how long they had been there or what they were doing there, but I came in with a smile on my face anyway.

"Hey, guys, what's up?"

"Nikki, think before you answer this question."

"Okay." I was a little concerned about Kyle's tone but tried to remain calm.

"A few days ago, a Mrs. Weatherby called and scheduled an appointment. She distinctly remembered talking with you because you two talked about her dog, Mr. Tompkins."

"Yes, I remember talking with her. She wanted to bring the dog, and it took me about 15 minutes to convince her not to."

"Okay, we have that established. Joel says that he put her paperwork in your basket to have you make some changes in her contract for him."

"Joel never gives me his stuff to type. He always gives it to Karan."

"He said that Karan was at lunch that day, and he needed it for his meeting today with Mrs. Weatherby and that he put it in your to-do basket with a note."

"If that were true, then I would at least have a copy of it in my done basket."

Karan moved aside to let me get to the basket. I looked through all the paperwork there and to my surprise, there it was under a whole bunch of documents. I looked at it incredulously.

"I never had this," I protested.

"Why would it be in your done basket?"

Kyle turned to Karan, "Do we have time to get this done before she leaves?"

"I'm on it; there are only a couple of changes that need to be made."

Then he looked at me with great disappointment and said, "I'll talk with you later."

They all left. I sat at my desk trying to remember getting that document. Robert came up the elevator and saw the look on my face.

"You don't look like someone who has just gotten their first car."

I told him what happened, and he got really upset.

"This has got to stop!"

He went down to Kyle's office and was in there about 15 or 20 minutes. When he came out, he said, "Kyle wants to see you."

He didn't look as upset as he had been when he went to his office, so I hoped everything was all right.

"Nikki, sit down."

And I did.

"You're doing an excellent job. I just want you to know that. I want you to think about the document that Joel says that he brought to you. Just think about it for a minute. Couldn't you just have forgotten he brought it to you?"

"No, Kyle, Joel has never brought me any of his work ever since I have been doing this. He has *always* taken it to Karan, no matter how pressing it was. I don't know if it is because he doesn't like me or if it is because he doesn't feel I can do the job adequately, but that's the truth.

"I put my initials on all of my work. If you check all of his work for the last couple of months against yours, you can tell what I have done opposed to what Karan has done."

"I see. Well, that is a good alibi. I'll check that out and get back with you."

"Can I go?"

"Yes."

I wanted to tell him that I saw Karan doing something earlier at my desk, but I didn't. I just left, and then Karan came out.

"Nikki, I hope that everything went okay with Kyle."

"Everything is fine."

She looked as if she didn't believe me.

"Really? Everything worked out OK?"

At that moment, Joel and Mrs. Weatherby came out of his office. He looked at us while we were talking. I continued talking to Karan as if everything was fine. By the time the evening mail came, however, I was truly ready to go home. It had been a good and bad day. George came through the office with a wide grin on his face.

"I see someone is having a wonderful day," I said.

Illegal Love | 95

"Yes, indeed."

He was about to pass my desk when he doubled back.

"Can you keep a secret?"

"Sure, does that mean that I can't even tell Robert?"

"I guess you can tell him."

"Okay, what is it?"

"I'm going to have a baby."

"Well, George, that is medically impossible."

"You know what I mean. Buffy is pregnant. Ever since we started going to the pre-marriage counselor, things have been much better between us."

"It's obvious that you are happy, so congratulations."

"Thank you, Nikki. I hope that you and Robert will feel this way one day."

"Maybe one day."

"By the way, I never told you that I think you two look great together."

I smiled. "Thank you, George."

He went on down the hall with a little bounce in his step. It was the first time I had any real acknowledgement that anyone cared what was going on in my life besides me and Robert. It pleased me that he approved. I went on and started working on the stuff in my to-do basket. Robert called me into his office, so I put everything to the side, went down the hall, and as a good receptionist, I knocked on his door. I learned from going into George's office that day I thought he was out, you don't just walk into someone's office unexpected because you never know what you might see.

"Come in."

I went in and sat down. He sounded serious.

"I need to tell you something."

I got concerned, and he must have seen it on my face.

"Oh, it's nothing too serious, but I want you to be careful. Kyle and I have to go out of town for 2 weeks, and I don't want you getting in any trouble with Karan and Joel while we are away. I'm going to make sure I have a long talk with Kyle before we go so that there won't be any misunderstandings about their position here—or yours."

"Okay. When will you be leaving?"

"Friday night."

I went over to where he was sitting, put my arms around his neck, and hugged him. I breathed in his aroma and told him that I would miss him at work—and at home.

"I know. I feel the same way. I wish I didn't have to go, especially with all the stuff that's going on right now, but I do."

"I don't want you to say anything to Kyle, but this morning when I came up, Karan was at my desk doing something."

"Why didn't you tell Kyle or me this earlier?"

"What good would that have done? She was just sitting there. That doesn't prove that she put that document there, right?"

"Well, I wish you would let me tell him."

"No, he'll just think that I'm using that as an excuse. I have to prove to him that it wasn't me."

"OK, I'll let you do this your way but—"

I put my fingers on his lips before he could finish speaking and said, "Baby, you can't fight all my battles."

"I know, but I want to try and help."

When I got back to my office, Kyle was there.

"Can I see you in my office?"

Karan's door was open. As we passed by, she looked up with this fake concerned look on her face. We stepped into his office, and Kyle turned to me and said, "Nikki, you're right. I hope that you accept my apology, and I will take care of this. I understand that not everyone in the office has to like each other, but they do have to respect each other or we can't be an effective team around here. I will not tolerate lying or trying to get one another in trouble. I'm going to have a talk with Joel and Karan to see what the problem is. Nikki, you do not have to worry about any repercussions from this, not even when I am away."

When I left the office, I walked slowly down towards my desk. I decided to act like things did not go well in my meeting with Kyle. When I got to Karan's office, I slowed my walk down even more. She came out of the office and asked, "Are you all right?"

With a sigh I said, "Yes, I hope so."

She put her hands on my shoulders and said, "We all make mistakes, but you will find that Kyle is a fair man—most of the time."

I went on to my desk and waited until Kyle called me.

"Have Karan and Joel come to my office, please."

"Yes, sir."

I made the phone calls. Karan came out and looked at me to see if I knew why he wanted her. I blinked my eyes and shrugged my shoulders. She walked down the hall. Joel came out of his office about the same time. They paused and then both went in. I called Robert and told him what was happening. He seemed pleased.

"You should have told Kyle about Karan."

"I'll call you back when they come out."

About 20 minutes later, Karan came stomping down the hall. Joel went into his office and slammed the door. Karan didn't slam hers, but she sure shut it hard. It was the funniest thing. I called Robert, told him, and he was laughing as hard as I was. By the end of the day, I was ready to go.

Robert and I decided that we would still ride together until the end of the week, then I would start driving my new car, new to me, that is. We went to our favorite Chinese restaurant for dinner. Mr. Wong was always so nice to us. Robert said that he had sent the restaurateur to a good tax lawyer one time and ever since then, he was just the nicest guy to him. We had our usual and as we always did, we sat on the same side of the table so that we could feed each other and sample each other's food. When I was full, I put my head on his shoulder.

"I'll miss you when you're gone."

"I'll call you every night and even during the day so it won't be like we're apart."

"Good, but I *will* know that we are apart because I won't have you sleeping next to me."

"Oh, I've taken care of that."

I looked up at him and asked, "How'd you do that?"

"Don't worry about it. I'll tell you later."

I thought, *Okay, but has he gone out of his mind?*

"Okay, daddy, whatever you say."

We stayed the night at his place and before we got ready for bed, he had me close my eyes. I did, and he turned off the lights. I heard some paper crunching and then he came back and sat on the bed.

"You can open your eyes now."

He turned on the lights and pulled something from behind his back. It was a big brown teddy bear and around its neck was a gold locket.

"Open it."

When I did, there was a picture of him in it on one side.

"The other side will be of you."

I couldn't stop the tears from coming.

"What's the matter?"

"You do too much for me."

"I do it because you are worth it, and I love you."

"Robert?"

"Yes."

"I love you, and your happiness is all that matters to me."

I hugged him so hard that if I were stronger, I would have hurt him. We kissed so passionately and for so long after that. I laid teddy on the floor, and we started to make love. Usually I would ask him to turn off the lights before I got undressed, but not tonight. Tonight I would have nothing to hide from this man that I loved, and that loved me too. But first, I stopped him.

"I need to tell you something." I leaned back against the headboard, and he sat in front of me.

"I need to tell you about some things from my past."

"Your past doesn't matter to me; I love you for who you are now."

"I know, but there are some things you need to know about me. Please don't say anything until I finish, or I might not be able to tell it all. It started around the time I first met my ex-boyfriend.

"I was working at a bank. This guy came from nowhere and wanted to cash a check, but he didn't have a driver's license. I told him that I couldn't cash it for him, but he said that he had been cashing checks at this bank before with just his picture ID from work, so I told him that I would have to let my supervisor see it. He said no problem, that it was fine with him. He even told me the supervisor's name. I smiled, and he said that he did this with every new person that got a job here.

"I did get his check approved and cashed it for him. He asked my name and I told him. Then he said that he'd see me next week, and he did. Every week he would come to my window.

"Then one day he asked me out. I didn't go right away, but he didn't stop asking. Finally, one day, I said yes. He was attractive, and he had a job. I'd been cashing the checks for him, Anthony Graham, for weeks. We went to dinner in a fancy restaurant, and I loved it. We soon became inseparable. He would come by at almost the same time every week to get his check cashed, and then we would meet after work and go out. Dinner, dancing, movies, plays, you name it.

"Then after about 2 months, he told me that he was having problems with his landlord. Something about him getting into it with a neighbor that was a relative of the landlord's. Well, the bottom line was he had to move. He told me that he didn't have that kind of money right then, so me, being who I am, told him that he could come and live with me, but just until he got enough money saved up."

I looked at Robert. He was just sitting there listening patiently. Hesitantly, I continued by saying, "Well, after a couple of weeks, I sort of noticed that he wasn't really leaving the house anymore. He would sometimes stay all day in the same clothes that he was in when I left for work, his nightclothes. He would always have an excuse about why he hadn't been looking for an apartment. His excuses changed almost daily. One day it was everything he looked at was too expensive or that they wanted too much deposit. I would just brush it off.

"Then one day while at work, I went to take some things into the bank manager's office and I saw that one of his checks had come back. It had some strange writing on it. My heart was pounding so hard. When I got home that night, I told him what I had seen. He said, 'Did they ask you anything about me?' I asked him why would they do that, but all he said, 'Don't worry about it, but if they do ask, just say you don't know anything. Just tell them I was a customer and you did get the checks approved from your supervisor, right?' Well, I had, and I started getting worried, but did nothing.

"The next day when I went to work, the bank manager called me into his office and asked me about the checks because my initials were on most of them. I told him that I had gotten permission to do so by my supervisor, Mrs. Pond. He said, 'We are not to take any more checks from this person, and if he comes into the bank again, alert security.' I told him that I would, and then left the office, grateful that I didn't have to lie about really knowing him.

"After work, I was really scared, because by now, he was using my car. He would pick me up in the afternoons, late, of course, but I thought it wouldn't be a good idea for him to be seen around the bank. When we got home, I told him what happened and asked him what was going on. He said that he had gotten into a fight with his boss and got fired because he ruffed him up a little bit. The man must have cancelled some of the checks.

"It didn't make sense to me, but I didn't want him to think I didn't trust him. I had to start taking the bus to work because he didn't want to go to the bank and he was using my car. Then one day when I got home, there were some guys at the apartment. Three really rough-looking guys. Anthony introduced them to me. He told me that one of them, Frank, was going to come into the bank tomorrow with his ID to cash a check, and that he was going to come to my counter and for me to just do my usual thing for him.

"I asked why he had to come to my window. He said, 'Because his ID will say Anthony Smith, and I need you to get it approved with your supervisor.' I told him that I couldn't do that. He hit me so fast I didn't realize it until I was getting up off the floor. The other guys just stood there looking, and one of them even had a smirk on his face. Anthony assured them not to worry about it, that I would be waiting for them. I went into the bedroom, afraid to cry in front of them. My lip was split and blood was everywhere. I wanted Anthony out, but now I was afraid to tell him.

"After that, things just got worse. Anthony began to hit me for any ole reason; it didn't matter: the food wasn't hot enough; the game he was watching was not going his way. It got to be where I was afraid to go in front of the TV because he would even kick me. Once I had to stay off work for a couple of days because otherwise, he said it would interfere with his money scam. Then these guys started coming in with bogus checks.

"Finally one day, I was called into the bank manager's office. He said that he had some concerns about some checks that I had been cashing lately. I told him that when I had any questionable checks, I had always gotten permission by my supervisor on duty. He told me that I should have been aware of the problems we were having with checks from that particular company. Beginning that day, I would no longer be working at a teller's counter; I would have to work in the back until further notice.

"When I went home, Anthony was packing. He told me that he got a job in California and that he had to leave immediately. Then he asked me how much money I had in the bank and forced me pull every dime I had. After that, he took me home and left—in *my* car. I was scared but glad to have him gone at the same time."

"And just like that, he was gone?"

"Yes, but that wasn't all. When I got to work the next day, there were some men in the bank manager's office, and he called me in. They placed me under arrest. I was taken to jail, fingerprinted, and had my photo taken. When I got into the interrogation room, those same two guys were there. They asked me a bunch of questions, and I told them the truth. I don't think that they really believed me until I showed them my back."

"What about your back?"

I turned around so that he could see it. There were whip marks all over it. Tears began flowing down his face.

"Anthony used to give me 'a lesson' at least once a week. He said it was just in case I got any ideas to go to the cops about what was going on. He had this long leather whip and would beat me like an animal. The more I cried, the more he hit me. It got so that after a while, I just kind of learned not to even whimper."

"How could I not notice this?"

"I didn't want you to see it, and most of the time, I would make sure your arms were not around me when we were naked."

"My poor baby." He looked as if he wanted to cry again, but he didn't.

"They didn't prosecute me, but I had to sign an agreement that I wouldn't work around money again, at least for the next 5 years, and they put me on probation for a year. By the time everything was done, I had lost my job, my apartment, my dignity, my car, and all my money. I only started feeling better about myself when I started working for the firm. I've lived in a shelter, and it was there that the women helped me. They helped me get a place to live and showed me programs I could go to for free to get back on my feet. I had worked at three other temporary jobs before coming to your firm, when I wasn't working at a fast-food restaurant or bartending."

That night we didn't make love. We just lay in each other's arms all night. Robert held me as I let everything out, and he told me that he loved me even more for being honest with him. All the pain of having everything bottled up inside me came out that night.

The next morning we got up in silence, but I knew that Robert had questions. I didn't want to bring it up myself, but I wanted him to feel comfortable with me and free to ask me anything. While driving, I said, "If you have any questions, Robert, please, don't hesitate to ask them. I don't want you to feel you have to walk on pins and needles around me."

"Honey, I don't understand how you could let someone come into your house like that."

I said, "Just like you started taking care of me without really knowing me, I was trying to help him."

"But why didn't you try to get some help when you saw what was happening?"

"I was scared, and then when he started using the whip on me, I got even more scared."

"I feel so bad for you."

"I know, but I've grown, and I've made a lot of progress to get myself back together."

"Yes, you have."

When we got to work, I went to my desk, and Robert went to his office. He kissed me ever so gently. Shortly after getting everything ready for the day, Karan came in. She didn't really look at me, she just sorta said good morning to the air. Without pausing, she went to her office and shut the door. I didn't let it faze me. George came in, still in his wonderful mood.

"How's Buffy?"

"She's fine. She's going through some morning sickness right now and not loving that at all."

"Well, hopefully, that will pass shortly."

"Yes, I can't wait."

He bounced all the way down to his office. Then I remembered that I had forgotten to tell Robert about the baby, so I knocked on his door.

"Just a minute. Come in."

I went into the office, trying to act as if everything was normal. He was sitting at his desk, although it didn't look like he was really working. A look of sadness was on his face, but I didn't want to acknowledge that it had anything to do with me. In my perkiest voice I said, "What were you doing in here? Playing with yourself?"

"What?!!"

"Nothing. Oh, I forgot to tell you that George and Buffy are having a baby."

In a dry sort of tone, he said, "That's good. I'm glad for them."

"Well, I thought that you would want to know," then I started out the door.

"Nikki, can I ask you something?"

I thought, *Here it comes. More questions.*

"Yes, dear."

He looked at me funny, then said, "Do you think that was his real name?"

"I did, until I was taken into custody. They didn't tell me what his real name was, but they told me that the name Anthony Graham, as I knew him, was an alias. Is there anything else?"

"No."

"Will we be having lunch together today?"

"Sure."

I went back to my desk to start doing my work, not sure of what Robert was feeling right now. I just wanted—and needed—to delve into my work. Shortly after I sat down though, Karan came and dropped some invoices on my desk, then walked away without a word.

"Karan, what's this?"

"Your boss wants you to know how to do that," she replied over her shoulder.

"Well, you can't just put this on my desk and expect me to know what to do with it."

"Oh, I thought that you would."

I knew then we needed to talk, so I jumped up and went into her office right after her.

"Excuse me, but are you having a problem with me today for some reason?"

"I would say yes, but I'm afraid that you'll go back to Kyle and tell him that I'm not respecting your space."

"And what is *that* supposed to mean?"

"To tell you the truth, I don't know what you said to Kyle, but he got all up in my ass yesterday about those documents."

"All I told him was that I don't handle Joel's stuff—you do—and I had a way of proving it; that was all. Would you like to have lunch with me?"

I think I caught her by surprise. She looked startled. In a quiet, none-Karan way she said, "Sure."

I walked back to my desk and called Robert and told him that I was planning on going to lunch with Karan.

"Really?"

"Yes, I think we need to get some ground rules established."

"I'll see you this afternoon, then. I have some things to do today before we leave anyway."

I hung up the phone and started looking at the invoices she had placed on my desk. I had no clue what to do with them and right now was not the time to ask Karan for assistance, so I put them down and started working on something else. Shortly after the mail came, I sorted it and then I called Karan to see if she was ready for lunch. She said that she was, and we went downstairs to the cafeteria. We sat at our usual spot, and I was kind of hoping that Niyokia and her friends would be there today. Before we started eating, I told her that I asked her down for a reason. She sat back in her chair, crossed her arms, and said, "Okay."

"I don't know how you're going to take this, but I feel like I must say it. I am *not* trying to take your job."

In a silly sort of tone, she said, "I know that."

"No, I don't think that you do. Hear me clearly, I am *not* trying to take your job, and I would appreciate it if you would let your brother know this, too, so he can stop trying to make mine so much harder than it is."

That said, I blessed my food and began to eat. She didn't move for a minute. She was just sorta stuck in that same position, with that same sorta stupid look on her face. Then she picked at her food for the next 30 minutes.

On the elevator going back to the office, I tried to make light conversation.

"I hope we all can get along for the 2 weeks that Kyle and Robert are gone," I said pleasantly.

She never said anything. When the elevator stopped at our floor, she just went towards her office, but she did say that she would be out soon to help me with the invoices. I called Robert on his cell phone. He had left a note saying that he was not in the office, that he was out taking care of some business. He finally answered on the third ring.

"How did your lunch go with Karan?"

"I hope that I have gotten my point across, but only time will tell."

"Okay, I'll see you when you get off."

"Bye, honey."

When I finished talking to Robert, I checked the message machine to see if there were any new appointments to be made. There were several, but the rest were personal calls for the associates. Patrick had called several times, specifically asking for Kyle to call him back as soon as possible. Then there were two calls for Robert that sounded personal, from a woman. I just transferred them all. I'm not the jealous type, but I could tell she tried to sound sexy. When Karan came out, I tried to make some more small talk.

"Karan, did you ever meet Robert's old girlfriend?"

"Sure, we all did."

"Oh?"

I wanted to ask her what she was like, but I really didn't want her to know that I was concerned. All I needed right now was for her to crank up the gossip mill about Robert and I having problems. I wondered if the woman who had called was his old flame.

Karan got me started on doing the invoices and then went back to her office. I thought if anyone knew anything, then it would be Niyokia. I didn't really want to go down there, but I was curious about what kind of person she was, so I put the answering machine back on, then went down to 620.

There was Niyokia, sitting at her big desk with her headset on, just talking like she didn't have a care in the world. She saw me when I got off the elevator, but it did nothing to slow down the chatter. Finally she stopped when I got near her desk.

"Girl, I'll call you back later."

"Hey, how are you doing, Niyokia?"

With a smirk on her face she said, "Fine. What can I help you with today?"

She was studying me, so I had to be careful. I knew if I said too much, I might live to regret it.

"Well, nothing much."

She shook her head and just looked at me. I took a deep breath, not believing that I was doing this, and said, "I know that you already know about Robert and me."

She said something like, "So what?"

"I have a question?"

"Okay, spit it out."

"Well, did you know his other girlfriend?"

Her eyes got wide. She came alive like someone had told her that she had won a million dollars.

"Well, I *do* know a little bit."

"Like what?"

"Not much really, except that she used him to get ahead at her company, and then she started dating her boss, who made more money than Robert did."

"That's terrible."

"Girl, yes, he did everything for her, too. Yeah, she was always coming up to that office for something or another. She shopped all the time, and as I heard it, he paid for most of it. It's a wonder that poor boy isn't broke by now. He used to send her flowers, and they were always taking trips to some exotic place or other. She was one of those sorority girls, and she was never really nice to any of us. She just considered us the hired help. Yeah, her and that Buffy girl are best friends."

My eyes got wide with curiosity.

"Yeah, he was about to propose to her when he found her with her boss. That poor boy must have gone through hell, but he never acted like anything other than a good lawyer. He didn't stop working; as a matter of fact, he started working *more*. A couple of the girls here thought that they could take his mind off of her, but none of them ever made it as far as you."

"What do you mean, 'as far as me'?"

"Well, he went out with one or two of them, but nothing serious— no rings, nothing but dinner, at least that's what I was told. They all said that he was courteous and kind, but that apparently there weren't any sparks flying."

There was a pause. Then she said, "Well, not until you."

"What do you know about me?"

"Well, girly, I know that he used to take you home a lot, then it stopped, but when it started back up, it *really* started back up. The rumor is he has found someone to take care of again."

"I can take care of myself!" She was making me hostile. *Did they really believe that he took care of me?*

"I'm sure of that, but isn't it nice to have a nice new lawyer boyfriend helping you get new things like a nice new apartment not too far from his?"

"How do you know about that?"

"This building is like a little community. Not many things go on without someone knowing about it, and I know most of it."

"Karan told you, didn't she?"

"Maybe, and maybe not, but what you have to understand is that we are all connected here. The same people that he knows might know someone that I know or might know someone that works here. You never know. And by the way, did you know that he is footing the other half of your rent? You don't think Mr. Robbins would just give you an apartment like that dirt-cheap, do you?"

"How do you know about that?"

"I'll tell you this and not much more. Most of the people that your lawyer boyfriend gets his favors from has either hired him or he has sent them to the big law firm upstairs, but one way or another, I know about it."

I turned to walk away, not wanting her to know how badly she had just hurt me so I just said, "Thanks for the info." She had some kind of power over the people in this building, and I did not want to become her enemy. Besides, she knew enough about my present life. I didn't want her knowing anything about my past. I don't think I'd be able to continue working here if that ever got out. I went back upstairs to a mess. Karan had been looking for me, and Tom had some paperwork he needed back real soon. He said, "Nikki, I put the papers on your desk earlier today with a sticky note saying 'please process immediately.'"

I was letting the little green monster of jealousy get to me. I tried to get caught up for the rest of the day, but all I could do was to think about what Niyokia had said. Robert had been "keeping me" and I was leaning on man for my support. I didn't want that to happen. If I slipped, I could end up right where it got me in the past. By quitting time, I had all of these different little scenarios running through my mind. Robert was going to get tired of the old abused girl. He would then get rid of me, and then I would lose my job, then my apartment, and then the car. And I would be left with nothing again. By the time I got to the car, I was scared, furious, mad, and tired. Too much brainwork in such a short period of time. When I got down to the car, I didn't want to talk to Robert.

"How was the rest of your day?"

I said nothing; I didn't want to speak to him.

"Did I do something to you?"

I just blurted it out. "When were you going to tell me that you were paying half of my rent?"

Startled, he looked over at me wondering that I knew and asked, "Who told you?"

"Does it matter?"

"No, I guess not. I just wanted you to get out of that hellhole, and I had done some work for Mr. Robbins, so we came up with an agreement that I felt we both could live with."

"Who's 'both'? You and Mr. Robbins?"

"Yes. I would do some extra work for him every now and again whenever he needed it, at a reduced rate."

"So, when were you going to tell me?"

"Never, really. I thought that you didn't need to know. I wanted you to feel like you were doing most of it on your own. I know how much independence means to you. Who told you?"

"It really doesn't matter. Robert, I need you to stop doing so much for me. If I don't do it on my own, I won't feel like I'm earning my way."

"I'm sorry; I should have talked with you first about it."

When I looked over at him, I could tell that he was really sorry for what he had done. I loved those eyes. I couldn't stay mad at him for long, although I wanted to.

"You're forgiven this time, but please consult me the next time you make a major purchase on my behalf. That especially means cars and such."

He smiled and gave me his best puppy-dog eyes and said that he would. I leaned over while he was still driving and kissed his cheek.

"Is that all I get for these eyes?"

I smiled, "Just wait until later."

We ended our day as we did most days, making love until we passed out and sleeping wrapped in each other's arms.

For the next few days, we barely let each other out of the other one's sight. Robert would be leaving me soon, and I needed every single moment possible with him. On Friday, I was so sad. He and Kyle had brought their things to the office because they were having a car pick them up. When they got ready to leave, they walked to the front of the building. I followed, wanting to see Robert every second that I could. He put his things in the trunk and came over to where I was standing. Then he held out his arms, and I ran to them.

"You'll be all right without me here, won't you?"

I poked out my lip. "No."

"You have to be a big girl or else teddy will feel left out."

"Well, then, send teddy away with Kyle."

He hugged me and then he gave me one of his sweetest kisses until Kyle said, "Man, you better come on; she'll be here when you get back."

I laid my head on his chest to listen to his heartbeat for one last time.

"I love you, and I *will* be here when you get back."

"I love you, too, and you better be."

He turned and got into the car. I stood there watching them drive off until I couldn't see them anymore. Then I slowly walked back into the building, and there was Niyokia on the elevator when I got on. She smiled at me, but I turned my back to her and punched my floor. Today would be the second day that I had driven my car. The weekend was long and quite boring. Teddy and me missed Robert so much. I didn't realize how much I depended on his presence.

On Saturday, he called, and we spoke for a couple of hours, talking about how much we missed each other but nothing major. On Sunday, I had to go over to his apartment and water the plants. I saw that his answering machine was blinking and without thinking about it, I listened to his messages. There she was again!

"Hey, Robert, it's me. Just returning your call. Give me a ring when you get this message."

Who the hell is this? It had to be her. I went home pissed. I beat up on teddy a little bit, but then I apologized to him. I told myself there was a rational explanation for her calls and that he would tell me when he got home. I just had to be patient. When he called, I didn't mention it, and we talked like nothing was going on.

He said, "Well, this is the countdown."

After our long conversation, I went to bed.

Chapter 8

The first couple of days without Kyle and Robert went off perfectly. Everyone walked around with a sort of quiet politeness, even Joel wasn't too bad. It was "thank you" this and "thank you" that, but by Wednesday, things were back to normal. Karan put a whole pile of work on my desk. I thought if I have to do all of this, what is *she* doing?

When I sorted the mail and took it around, to my surprise, Joel had decided to play musical chairs with his in-box. I just put it on his desk. He wasn't in his office, so I figured I would hear about it later on in the day.

As lunch approached, I wanted something different from the cafeteria food, but I was reluctant to go too far, so I ended up going downstairs anyway. I hit the mother lode. Karan, Niyokia, and some ladies were sitting down having their lunch in their usual spot and so would I. There was Karan, running her mouth again. She was going on about how that "little twit"—meaning me, I assumed—was just hanging onto her job by a thread.

"She's sleeping with Robert, and for all I know, she could be sleeping with more of them. Girls, you just don't know—she is *always* messing up something, and I have to go back and correct it. It's like the work has to be done twice. And you know that Robert is almost tired of her. It's just a matter of time before he gets enough of that 'sweet innocent' routine of hers. You know, 'Oh, I'm so helpless, pay for my apartment,' and guess what? She drove to work today in a *car*. I bet you anything he bought it for her. You all know how kind he is. Remember that other little twit he dated?"

Illegal Love | 111

I sat in amazement hearing about my life that way, and she said all of this before she took her *first* bit of her meal.

Someone said, "Karan?"

"What?"

"Didn't you try to date Robert once?"

"Not really. I knew that he was going through a hard time, so I fixed him a couple of home cooked meals at my place. That's all."

Niyokia said, "I think I recall you getting mad one week about him refusing to come to your place after the second time."

Everyone started laughing. Karan said quickly, "Oh no, it wasn't like that at all. It was just he didn't want to confuse our relationship at work."

Someone said, "He sure didn't confuse his relationship with that pretty receptionist though."

Karan retorted, "Well, you know some men will do *anything* for a piece of ass."

Someone else mumbled, "Well, not for a piece of yours, it seems."

Niyokia rolled and then she just burst out laughing. Then they all caught on, at least everyone except Karan. She just said, "Well, we were friends, and I was not trying to go there with him."

Niyokia snickered, "Okay, if that's what you want us to believe. I just know that most of the girls around here tried and failed."

She was about to say something else and my heart sank. I thought she was going to tell them about me coming to see her last week, but she didn't. I held my breath for a little bit longer, then I sneaked out. I went upstairs, furious that Karan would be lying to all those women but then, why was I surprised? She was threatened by me, and I suspected that Robert was only one of the reasons. In a little while, she came up, not looking too happy by the earlier events. Straightaway she walked to my desk.

"Did you go to lunch?"

With a sort of blank expression on my face, I replied, "Yes, I did, in the cafeteria."

"Oh, so did I. I didn't see you."

She quickly turned to go into her office. Before reaching her room, she looked back at me and saw that I was still watching her. For the rest of the day, she didn't come out of her office.

By the end of the week, things were just okay. There had been some ups and downs, but nothing major happened. Karan made an attempt to be nice; she even brought me a small teddy bear to sit on my desk with sad eyes. He was holding a sign that said, "I Miss You When You're Not Here."

"Thanks."

"No problem. I just thought that you would be missing Robert, and I hope the bear will help."

I wanted to believe her, but past experiences made me think twice about anything she did for me, nice or not. She also invited me to a party, but I declined the invitation. I had planned on spending the weekend talking to Robert on the phone and checking on his plants. When I got home, I got ready for bed and picked up my new bestseller book that I had started reading last week, *HER TWO LOVES*, by Felicia Truttier. I was really into it when Robert called.

"What are you doing?"

I was glad to be on the receiving end of that deep, sexy voice. He reminded me of what a younger Barry White must have sounded like talking on the phone.

"Sitting here trying to read so I won't think about how much I miss you," I replied.

"I miss you, too. Well, one more week, and it's all over with, and then I'll be home in your arms forever."

"Well, don't swell my head. There'll be other trips, and you will have to leave me again."

"Yes, but I will always come back to you."

We talked more about what he was doing on his trip and then we said our I love yous and hung up. I missed him so very much. I curled up with my novel and kept reading until sleep came. On Saturday, I went around and did some shopping. Then I went to Robert's to check on his plants; of course, this time, I checked the answering machine on purpose. The message was gone, which meant that he had called and retrieved it, and there wasn't a new one. I did what I was supposed to do then I left and went home. By Monday, I was on the brink of cracking. I wanted Robert back, and I wasn't going to be happy until he was here. Buffy came to see George, and they spent most of the morning locked up in his office. I was so jealous. When they came out, she tried to be sociable.

"Has George told you the good news?"

"Yes, and I am so happy for you two."

Illegal Love | 113

"Maybe soon you can be this happy. I love everything so far, except for the morning sickness, but George is a sweetheart, even trying to make that as painless as possible."

She looked as if she had been changing, maybe growing inside a little, and I was happy for them. When she left, I felt that maybe one day we might become friends.

When I saw Karan, I figured that she would tell me how the party went, but she didn't. I went down to the cafeteria for lunch by myself. There I found Niyokia and her bunch, so I sat next to them.

Niyokia was laughing. She had such a happy laugh too. She was saying, "No way" to one of her friend's remarks.

I leaned closer. One of the girls was saying, "When I got to the party, Karan tried to act like she was the big shit. She walked in, speaking to folks that didn't speak to her. Then she spent most of the night chasing Patrick and him running from her. He even looked surprised that she was there."

Niyokia laughed. "She had come down asking me if I wanted to go to his big party, but I told her that my man and I had plans."

The other girl that was talking said, "Well, I guess that's when she got me, saying that she would introduce me to him and that they were special friends, but no one knew about it. After the party, I thought that *he* must not have known about it either."

They all laughed so loud you would have thought they were having their own party. I wanted to laugh myself, but I thought it would not be nice because just last week, I was the subject chewed on for the lunch menu. I just finished my meal and left.

When I reached the office, I went to Karan's room.

"Hey, how was the party this weekend?"

"Well, I didn't go; I forgot I had made other plans," she lied.

"Oh, well, maybe you'll make the next one."

I closed the door and went back to work, shaking my head. Later on during the week, her mood got a little better, but not much.

Thursday night finally arrived. I was so excited about Friday that I forgot to ask Robert what time they were coming back, but I knew that I would wait up all night on them if that was what it took. When I woke up, I wasn't sure what I wanted to wear; I wanted to look sexy, but not too sexy for work. I wanted Robert to say, "Now *that* is what I've been looking forward to" when he saw me. I finally picked something nice to wear. In the garage at work, I saw Joel and Karan had ridden in together.

I wondered if something was wrong with his car. I know that they saw me, but they both acted like they didn't and kept to themselves. They even let the elevator door close on me. I shook my head in disgust and told myself that things were back to normal. When I got to the office, they hadn't even turned the lights on.

I did my usual morning stuff and awaited my boss and my lover. Mail came, lunch went, and mail came again, but no Kyle or Robert, not even a phone call. I was growing terribly impatient. I went to Karan, Tom, and George to see if anyone had heard when they were due back. By the end of the day, everyone was leaving, and I was *still* sitting here waiting.

Before Karan left she said, "How long do you think you're going to be here?"

"I have a few things to finish up before I leave."

She had lied to me earlier in the week, and I didn't care if I lied to her now.

I was just getting ready to leave when the elevator opened up. It was Robert. I ran to his arms and gave him the biggest kiss ever. We stood there for what seemed like forever, just kissing. Then we got his things and took them into his office. He closed the door, turned on the lights, we dropped his bags on to the floor and went at each other like teenagers in heat. He leaned me up against the wall and lifted up my skirt. As he felt for my underwear, I reached for his belt buckle. I wanted his things off as much as he wanted mine off. I found his, he found mine, and there we were in each other's embrace for an hour or so. When we finished, I just wanted to sleep.

"I have a few things to do before we go," he said.

Both of us went to the restroom to freshen up. When we came back into his office, I lay on the sofa as he listened to his messages. Then he made some phone calls. I only half listened to them until he called some woman named Marilyn. I thought that maybe she was the woman who had been calling him. I *know* he wasn't calling her in my face.

He said to her, "Hey, I'm back. I got your call. What's up?"

He must think that I'm asleep over here.

He said, "I know you've been calling, but I was out of town for 2 weeks. Whatever it was that you needed, I couldn't take care of anyway until I got back. Oh, really? Well, I'm back now. OK, I'll see you on Monday then."

Illegal Love | 115

He hung up the phone and come over to me to give me a wake-up kiss. In a sarcastic tone I said, "I'm not asleep."

"Okay, are you ready to leave?"

"Yes, I guess so."

"Are you upset with me for some reason?"

"Did you think that I was asleep?"

"No, not really. Why?"

"Well, you were so wrapped up in your conversation."

He started laughing. I had never seen him laugh so hard. His pearly whites were glistening. Then he got to holding his stomach and just couldn't stop laughing. Well, let me tell you, this only aggravated me more.

"*What* is so funny?" I demanded.

"You're jealous."

"I am not."

"Yes, you are."

And then he started tickling me. I was so mad, but I couldn't help it. I started laughing with him. We rolled around a little and then got ready to leave.

On the way home, I was still a little upset because he had not addressed who Marilyn was. Finally I broke the silence by saying, "So, are you going to tell me who she is or what?"

He started laughing again, but this time I was not going to participate.

"Well?"

He wiped his eyes and said, "Marilyn is a client that calls a lot. I'm not sure if you have spoken with her, but she likes to flirt. It's all innocent. We kid each other back and forth. She's nearly 60."

"Why does she have your home number?"

"Because she owns a black art shop and that's where I got most of my artwork from at a discounted price."

I tried to put on my best sad face. "I'm sorry."

"How did you know that she called my house?"

I immediately thought up a lie.

"Well, when I was over watering the plants, the phone rang, and I heard the answering machine pick it up."

"Oh."

We pulled up to his place and took everything upstairs. After we put everything away, we made love again. Our passionate embrace just reassured me of the love we had for each other. We lay there together holding one another. Quietly, Robert said, "I didn't think that I was going to be able to last for 2 whole weeks without you."

Even lying down, he towered over me. He gently kissed me on the top of my head as he told me how he lay in bed at the hotel at night wishing that I were there with him. I loved him more right at this moment. I rolled over on top of him and said, "I'm hungry."

"How about Mr. Wong's?"

"I don't care, just as long as it's food."

I showered and then went looking for him; he was on the phone. He motioned for me to be silent and to stay away. I got a little concerned, but then I pushed the thought out of my mind. He had reassured me of his commitment. I had no reason to be jealous anymore. I figured he was talking with a client and didn't need to be distracted. I walked into the bathroom and finished getting dressed. He came in, hugged me from behind, lifted me up, and kissed the back of my neck continuously.

"Boy, are we in a good mood. Maybe you should leave me more often."

"If that's what you want."

"Shut up and take your shower."

He let me down and got into the shower. After we got to Mr. Wong's, he said, "I'll be right back."

I went over to our table. As I waited, I looked over the menu. Shortly afterwards, Robert came back with a huff and sat next to me.

"Where were you?"

"I had to go to the restroom."

"All that time you spent in the bathroom at your place, you could have done that while you were home."

"What are we going to have today?"

"Anything your heart desires."

He kissed me gently.

"My man is wonderful before he leaves, and then he's more wonderful when he gets back," I smiled.

We ordered some rice, chicken, and soup, then we talked about the work he did while he was out of town with Kyle. He told me about how Kyle kept trying to get him to go to these strip clubs and that all he could think of was me.

"Okay, really, how many did you go to?"

We laughed and talked as if we had never been apart and never would be again. I loved him, and the look in his eyes when he looked at me told me the same thing. We finished our meal and waited for our waiter to bring the bill. When he came, Robert gave him his credit card and he handed us two fortune cookies as usual on a tray. As always, I opened mine first. I closed my eyes and did my best swami impersonation and said,

"The lady's fortune for the day says ..."

Then I broke the cookie open and read the message: "WILL YOU MARRY ME?"

"Now isn't that funny?" I laughed.

Then Robert said, "Okay, open mine since you're so good."

I hadn't noticed that his cookie was slightly heavier than mine was.

I did the swami interpretation again and said, "The gentleman's fortune for the day says ..."

And when I broke it open, there was a *huge* diamond ring inside. Robert looked at me, as I looked at him. He took it out of my hands, knelt down on the ground, and said, "Your fortune cookie says will you marry me. Will you?"

With tears streaming down my face, I leaned over and said, "Yes. A million times, yes."

He kissed me so softly and put the ring on my finger. I couldn't imagine how he had possibly gotten the cook to do that. Everyone in the place stood up and clapped. Robert stood up and took a bow as I held my hand out and examined my finger. He sat back in the booth with me, then Mr. Wong and his family and some of the other waiters came out with a beautiful, small, white, wedding cake with a lit sparkler in the middle of it. They said, "Congratulations to our two favorite customers."

I was the happiest I had ever been in my life. The rest of the weekend was wonderful. We did absolutely nothing but lie around, make love, make more love, and make even more love. By Monday morning, I needed a rest from the weekend.

Chapter 9

On Monday morning, I couldn't wait to get to work. I didn't want to brag, but I wanted someone to share my joy with, even if it had to be Karan. In my heart, I wished that my mother were alive so that I could share this with her, or even if I knew how to get in touch with my father, for that matter. But for so many years, there had only been me, and now, I would have my own family. We drove up and on the way to the elevators, I saw Karan, and as usual, she tried to ignore me, but today, I wasn't having it. I made Robert quickstep with me so that we could catch the elevator with her. She spoke, but it was bland.

I asked, "How was your weekend?"

"Oh, it was fine."

Then she said it: "And how was yours?"

"It was wonderful," and I lifted up the 3.5 carat, perfectly formed solitaire daintily perched on my finger. Her eyes almost exploded out of her head. She put on one of her best fake smiles and hugged me, then said, "Congratulations to the two of you."

Robert nodded his head with a huge smile and said, "Thank you."

"Girl, I was so surprised when it all happened," I told her.

She said, "I bet."

When the elevator stopped, she was the first one to walk off. She went straight to her office and did not stop for anything. Of course, she shut the door. I kissed my fiancé on the mouth really hard.

"I'll see you later."

He went to his office, but not before saying, "Nikki, don't brag. You know it's going to be all over this building in about 2 seconds."

With an innocent wide-eyed expression, I replied, "Who, me?"

He smiled, went into his office, and closed the door.

For the next 2 days, I could hardly do anything without looking at the rock on my finger. By the third day at lunchtime, everyone in our building knew and had congratulated us, even Joel had given me his grunt of approval, at least, that was the way I took it. Kyle came by the desk once and said, "You won't believe how hard it was for the two of us to find the perfect ring and then to find someone to put it into a fortune cookie—now *that* was a task."

It made me very proud that my boss thought that much of me to help with a task that would make me the happiest woman on earth. On our way out to lunch, Kyle said, "Patrick is having a party, and that would be the perfect place for you to have your first outing as a newly engaged couple."

We told him that we would think about it. During lunch, I sat mesmerized, looking into the face of the man who was making my most desired and precious dreams come true. I didn't know what on earth I could ever do to make him understand just how lucky and loved I felt. He kept stopping during our meal, saying, "Will you *please* stop looking at me that way."

"What way?"

"I don't know, but just stop it."

"You know you are just one handsome-assed fella."

"Nikki, I love you, but sometimes you make me feel uncomfortable."

"Really? How?"

"I think you put me too high on a pedestal."

"Me?"

"We both have faults, and you make me feel so wonderful, and that is why I do the things that I do."

"Then you should realize why I look at you this way then. Before I came to this job, I was barely making it, and look at me now. Robert, a lot of it comes from what you've helped me to accomplish. I don't just feel gratitude, but admiration and love as well."

"I only did what I thought would make you happy."

"And so you have."

As I ate, I kept looking at my ring. It sparkled without any help from the lights above. I had never owned anything so beautiful in all my life, but I thought at that moment, he could have given me a bubble-gum ring and I would have been just as happy.

We ate our meal and then went back to the office. When we arrived, there were congratulation balloons all around my desk. I was thrilled. The guys and Karan came out and said it was the least that they could do. I hugged everyone except Joel, who did not bother to come out to the celebration.

Tom seemed a little teary-eyed as I kissed him on the cheek. Even Karan seemed to be nicer for the moment. I knew by now that the whole building knew about our engagement. Leaving the office at the end of the day, we got a lot of stares with all those balloons we carried to the car. We went to Robert's apartment, but I knew that tonight, I must spend my night alone. He had work to do, and we both knew he would not get much work done if I were there. After I gathered my things, I drove home. We talked on the phone for a while, then I curled up with my book and teddy.

By Tuesday morning, I was still ecstatically happy. Wednesday, Thursday, and Friday everything went wonderfully. Maybe I was just in a good mood and whatever did happen didn't bother me, and things ran like clockwork. Even Buffy seemed happy for us—or maybe not; I really didn't care. By Friday, Kyle had made us promise that we would attend Patrick's party.

Chapter 10

Saturday started out as a most wonderful day. I woke up to the smell of bacon frying, eggs, grits, toast, and coffee. I rose with a smile on my face and not just from the passion from the night before. In a cheery voice, I said, "You are wonderful."

"Don't you dare get out of that bed," Robert replied.

I smiled and said, "But I *have* to use it."

"Okay, then go ahead, but then you get right back into bed."

I jumped out of the bed, ran into the bathroom, used it, brushed my teeth, then ran back to the bed.

"Okay, I'm here."

He came in shortly with a tray full of food and a single rose and placed the tray on the table next to me.

"Good morning, my sweet."

"Oh, honey, you shouldn't have."

"I know, but I wanted to do something special for my wife-to-be."

"If I can expect this every Saturday morning, I'll marry you tomorrow."

With a chuckle and a wink he said, "Don't count on it."

I leaned forward and tenderly kissed him.

"Well, the next time you stay over at my house, I'll have to cook for you."

He did his best little boy routine. "But we hardly ever stay at your house," he pouted.

"Yeah, I know."

121

"You kidder; I'll fix you."

"You will, will you?"

"Yes, then you will just have to move in here with me."

"Robert?"

"What? You are here most of the time anyway."

My attitude changed to serious. I remembered what I heard Karan say, that he was taking care of me already and if I moved in now, he definitely would be in control of my life.

"Let's wait a little while. I still have to get used to the fact that we're going to be married."

"Really? I was used to that the day you said yes."

"You kidder."

I sat back as he fluffed up my pillows and sat the tray down over my lap. Breakfast was delicious. Robert was an excellent cook. After breakfast, we did some chores around the house then went out to run some errands. When we finished, he dropped me off at my place so that I could get dressed. In a couple of hours, he came back to pick me up and we were on our way once again.

When we got to the party, as usual, it was already crowded. Patrick's Saturday parties always seem like they were a continuation from what was a Friday party and would probably carry over to a Sunday party. People were everywhere. Celebrities, non-celebrities, people I recognized, and a lot I didn't. I told Robert under no circumstance was he to leave me alone, and he agreed.

We walked around. He talked to people that he knew and was always the gentleman, introducing me as his fiancée. Everyone was polite, but they could tell I was out of place. In the last couple of months of being with him, the way I dressed had improved. And I was working on my etiquette, but these people had been in money for a long time, their wives and girlfriends were jewel-bedecked, and they could smell an outsider from a mile away. I clung close to Robert.

Soon we spotted Kyle and Tom, so we went over near them. Kyle was standing with a kind of plain-looking woman, who was quiet and seemed shy. She didn't look like the type of women he would surround himself with and I wondered why he was with someone like that, especially tonight. He said, "Nikki, I don't think you have ever met my wife, Katherine."

Stunned, I said, "No, I haven't."

I smiled as I shook her hand. Her touch was gentle, and she lowered her eyes after we shook hands, as if she were aware of what I was thinking. Tom was alone. He said, "My wife wasn't feeling too well, so she stayed home."

I said, "I hope it's nothing serious."

"Oh no, she'll be fine, but she was not up for a crowd."

"I understand."

I stood near Kyle and his wife as Robert and Tom started talking. Kyle said, "Kate, I don't know if I told you that Nikki and Robert just got engaged."

She said, "No, honey, you didn't."

Her voice was as gentle as her appearance. I just could not get over seeing him with someone like that. She could have been beautiful, I guess, but something was missing.

George and Buffy showed up. I hadn't realized how big she was getting. It was a little funny seeing her like this, because she was still trying to wear skimpy clothes. A lady accompanied them, and everyone looked strange and awkward when she appeared. They greeted her, but in a sort of bland, distant kind of way. Robert just stood there for a moment before he turned and put his arms around me. She gave him this sly sort of smile when she looked at him, raised an eyebrow, and said, "Hello, Robert, you're not going to speak?"

He just looked at George and Buffy with a very *I'm-going-to-get-you* kind of stare and then answered, "Hello, Etowah."

She smirked, "Now, isn't that better?"

He said, "Nikki, this is Etowah."

She smiled as I held out my hand to shake hers, and then she saw my ring. At first, she almost didn't take my hand.

I said, "Hello, nice to meet you."

Her expression had turned to cold shock as she said, "Same here."

She almost snatched her hand away from mine. I knew from that action who she was. I looked up at Robert, he looked down at me, then he said, "Come on, baby, let's go get something to drink."

As we walked over to the bar, he apologized.

"For what?" I asked.

"I didn't want you to see her or anything."

My Robert, who, for the last year that I had known him, had been nothing but calm and cool now seemed out of sorts. I lifted my hand to his face and said, "Baby, there is *nothing* for you to apologize for. We

124 | *Felicia Fruttier*

are together now and believe me, I am no longer jealous of anyone, *especially* her."

"Thank you," he said humbly, then he kissed the hand that lay on his cheek.

"Stay here, honey. I want to talk with George, but I'll be right back, I promise."

"Don't be mad at him. He probably didn't have anything to do with this."

"Maybe, but I want to know what happened and why."

"Please don't be long."

"I won't. Promise."

I stood there watching him as he walked over and touched George on his shoulder. Then they walked away. From were I stood, I could see her clearly. She was tall and slender, but not skinny. She was sorta hippie, and her shape seemed almost perfect to me. Her hair was long and sandy-colored, the kind you would try to get from a bottle, but which would never turn out right for you—but, of course, *hers* was perfect. Her skin was as flawless as a ripened peach in a picture-perfect garden. When I was close to her, I could tell she didn't need makeup, even though she had a little bit on. Her chocolate-brown eyes instantly drew you in and hinted at secrets, and her full, red lips were formed in a sassy half-smile on her face. Even her voice was perfect. She purred in a soft, coquettish drawl. The only thing that I saw that could have been seen as an imperfection was her nose. For some reason, it appeared to be slightly too big for her face, but then I thought I could just be looking for something—*anything* out of place. I looked at this gorgeous creature, who could have easily been a model or actress, and thought how Robert must have hated losing her—and then to end up with someone like me. By then, I wanted to go home!

Darkness clouded my thoughts, and then it seemed as if Robert had been gone forever and since I needed to use the restroom, I went looking for one. The line was too long in the downstairs bathroom in the house, but I remembered that Patrick had a pool and there was probably something down there. I thought I would sneak out and use that one. When I got there, it was deserted, and boy, was I glad because by now, I was doing the pee-pee dance.

Having to go so badly, I had not noticed the small one-bedroom studio by the pool, but coming out of the cabana feeling much relieved, I could tell that someone was living there, and I got afraid that I had

Illegal Love | 125

invaded their privacy. Moving back towards the house at a faster pace, I was crossing the pool area, and someone caught me by the waist.

"Oh, Robert, what took you so long?" I asked.

He turned me around, and I almost choked. I started coughing and could not stop. He said, "Nikki, Nikki, Nikki."

I pulled away so quickly I almost fell.

"I was hoping that I would see you again, baby."

I tried to walk away, and he came closer. I thought, *Oh my God, where is Robert?* The more I moved away, the closer he came.

"Nikki, are you running? Don't you remember I don't like to chase? Wasn't that one of our little lessons?"

"Please," I begged.

"Please what? I told you I would never hurt you."

I thought if I ran away really fast, I might be able to find Robert before he could catch me, or maybe he wouldn't chase me because of all the people milling around, but the fear was more powerful than I was. I knew I had to do something. I turned, and when I did, Robert was right there. I called out to him. He saw me. I had hoped this would scare Anthony away. Robert walked over to me with a strange look on his face. I thought that he must have seen us, and that I would have to explain. He came up and put his hand on my waist, and I sort of fell into him.

"Are you alright?" he asked.

"Yes, I am now."

Robert took a deep breath and then said, "Hello."

I couldn't breathe.

He continued, "So, you're still here?"

I turned around and got the shock of my life. There was Robert standing next to Anthony, and they were almost identical. My heart skipped a beat. Robert pulled me close to him.

"Nikki, I want you to meet my brother, Noel."

"Your brother? Noel?" I repeated the questions back to him; I couldn't believe what I was seeing—let alone what I was hearing.

"Yes, do you two already now each other?"

My Anthony—his Noel—replied with a "No." He had a sneaky grin on his face.

Then Robert said, "Noel, I would like for you to meet my future wife."

Noel—Anthony—whoever he was—reached down and grabbed my hand and looked at the engagement ring.

"Congratulations," he said dryly.

I stood there limp as a noodle.

Noel then said, "Brother, you've been busy up here, with all your money and your important friends."

Robert said, "Noel, please don't start."

"No, I won't air our dirty laundry in front of your fiancée; I'll wait until you tie the knot."

"Why are you still here?"

"Well, it seems that Patrick needs someone to be here to watch over the place sometimes when he's away, and, well, that's where I fit in. And you know this isn't a bad place to live for free."

"Please don't take advantage of Patrick. He has enough problems, Noel."

"I know he does, and don't you forget, I'm the reason you get paid for them."

"I can't talk to you. You haven't changed at all, Noel."

Robert took my arm, and we walked away. I could barely move my knees by now. They knocked, my legs wobbled, and I felt as if I would faint at any moment.

"Robert, I really don't feel well. I need to go home."

"I want to go also, but we promised that we would be here for a little while."

"I know, but I can't."

Just then, I vomited up everything I had eaten that day. Robert grabbed me, and I went down. It was awful to be the center of attention. Everyone stopped whatever they were doing and turned to watch the sideshow. Kyle, Tom, George, Buffy, and, of course, Etowah, came rushing over. They all asked if I was okay.

Robert said, "Yes, she wasn't feeling well; we were just about to leave."

Buffy's thoughtless selfishness came out as she said, "Maybe she's pregnant, like me."

Robert fixed her with a cold stare as she stuffed her face, then he helped me up. He and Tom escorted me out to the front. Then Tom stayed with me until Robert brought the car around. As he drove off, I apologized.

"Honey, it wasn't your fault. It was probably my brother's fault."

"How would you know that?"

"The way he acts makes *me* sick sometimes."

I leaned my head out the window as he drove. I needed as much air as possible. When we got back to his place, I asked for a drink, but he said, "No, you're in no condition to be drinking."

I cleaned up and went to bed. Neither one of us were in a mood to make love, and I was glad. I was so restless that I hardly slept. Nightmares invaded my dreams. I would roll over and hug Robert, but then I would get scared because I thought it was Noel. Finally, I got up, poured myself a glass of water, then went into the living room, and that's where I stayed until dawn.

When Robert woke up that morning, I was still there, wide-awake. He came into the living room calling my name, but I said nothing. I just sat there. Concerned, he came and knelt down in front of me.

"Nikki, have you been up all night?"

"I had nightmares, and I couldn't sleep."

"Oh, honey, I think I know what the problem is."

I looked at him. "Really?"

"Yes, but you don't have anything to worry about. I love you. Etowah was my past, and you are my future."

I leaned down and kissed the top of his head as he had so often done to mine.

"Yes, my darling. Everything will be all right."

He laid his head on my lap and said, "I want you to move in with me. I don't want you to have to go home; I want *this* to be your home all the time."

"Yes, my darling."

I stared into the blankness of my mind as I rubbed his head. He continued. "Then we can plan the wedding, and we'll never be apart again."

I moved around in a daze all day, thinking that I should be doing something but what, I did not know. Robert worked on some cases, while I just stared blankly at the TV. Occasionally he would come over and see if I was all right. I wanted to just lie down and cry, but how would I explain that to Robert? He thought all of this was because of some skinny ex-girlfriend of his. How could I explain to him that my nightmare had a name, and it also had a brother that I loved? I got up and told him that I needed to go home. He was wonderful. He said

OK, just like that. He didn't even question my reason; he just stopped what he was doing and drove me home.

When I got there, I couldn't even do what I thought I needed to do. I couldn't cry. The scenarios started though. What if I tell him the truth? They don't get along anyway, but people say that blood is thicker than water. What if I made him realize that I didn't even know his brother's real name until last night? Then he would think me a fool letting someone take over my life like that, and I didn't even know who he was. What to do? Well, one thing was certain. I didn't have a clue. The only thing I did know was that last night was just the beginning.

Chapter 11

Monday morning when Robert called and said he was on his way, I told him to go on, that I would be right behind him. After I hung up the phone, I lay back down again. I was so tired. It was another sleepless night. Memories of the beatings haunted me. I had lived for almost a year and a half without really thinking about it or thinking about Anthony/Noel. I had felt that God had forgiven me for the mistake I made with him and had blessed me with Robert. But now, what about now? I closed my eyes for what seemed like only moments, then my phone rang. It was Robert.

"Baby, are you all right?"

"I'm on my way."

"It's 10:00. I talked with you hours ago."

I jumped up. "It can't be!"

"Yes, but I've talked to Kyle and told him that you were still sick from this weekend, and he said it was fine, that you should just stay in bed today."

"I'm so sorry."

"It's okay, but I'm worried about you. I'll be over after work."

"Okay."

We hung up the phone. I lay back down, and that's where I was when Robert came through the door. The lights were off. He hurried to my room and found me asleep, curled up with the phone still in my hand. He kissed me gently on my cheek, and I woke up.

"When did you get here?"

"Just now."

129

"What time is it?"

"It's 7:00."

"A.M.?"

"No, P.M."

I could not believe that I had slept that long.

"I even stopped by my place to pick up some things."

I sat up, and then he sat at the end of the bed.

"Baby, you have got to let this go."

"What are you talking about?"

"Etowah."

"Oh, I'm not thinking about that."

"Then tell me what's wrong."

"Nothing's wrong; I just haven't been feeling good!" I protested.

"Do you think that you're pregnant?"

"Robert, my cycle is more on time than you are with your clients."

"Well, then, help me understand what's going on with you."

"I just don't feel well right now."

"If you need a couple of days off, I can talk with Kyle, and we could go away for a long weekend."

"Maybe later."

I got up and went into the bathroom to freshen up. "Have you eaten?" I asked.

"No."

"Good. Let's get something. I'm starving."

We went down to The Pizza House. As we sat and ate, Robert started telling me stories about him and his brother, Noel.

"Baby, I'm telling you these things not because I want to scare you off, but because I want you to know that I love you and I have nothing to hide from you."

"Why didn't you tell me you had a brother?" Even if I would have known, it would not have helped me now, because I would not have gotten the connection.

"Well, most of the time, I don't think about Noel. He only comes around when he's in trouble or he needs some money. Those are really the only times he comes to see me."

"And when do you look for him?"

"I don't. You wouldn't understand."

I understood more than he realized. He took a bite of his pizza, wiped his mouth, and started his story.

"For some reason when we were growing up, my brother wanted to go live with my aunt when my parents died. My grandmother was already elderly when we came, and she did not oppose the move. I never really knew why he wanted to do that."

I looked closely at Robert to see if he would be alright telling me his story. He seemed OK and then continued.

"My brother and Aunt Jay moved around a lot. My grandmother could never keep up with them, and even though Noel may not know this, or doesn't want to admit it, my grandmother tried terribly to get back custody of him, but was never able to keep up with them.

"When I was about 16, Noel showed up on our doorsteps. He looked like he had been beaten up pretty badly. My grandmother was really old by then, but she took him in anyway. I almost didn't recognize him. I hadn't seen him in almost 10 years. When I found out who he was, I so glad. I had my brother back. I thought things would be great, that we would become best friends. I would introduce him to all of my friends, and they would like him because, well, he was my brother.

"It took a couple of days for him to heal, but when he got well, Granny put him in the school with me. He wasn't adapting well, though. I was in most of the sports and knew a lot of people. He wasn't interested in doing those things, but I thought it was okay, if that's what he wanted. I still introduced him to my friends, but soon, they didn't like him, and he didn't like them. He started hanging with the kids that smoked and cut classes. Soon Granny found out and said that if he was going to live under her roof, he would have to try to do better. He didn't listen to her, and then one day, she got another call that he had skipped school. When he came home, she was furious. She fussed and fussed, and he kept telling her to leave him alone and was very disrespectful.

"I was in the living room doing my homework. I kept hearing her fuss and I kept hearing him yell at her and telling her that she didn't know what she was talking about. Granny was stern, and she was relentless. She would not stop until she knew that you understood what she was trying to say. So the more he walked away from her, the more she followed him, and then she must have touched him. I don't believe she was trying to hit him because she had never laid a hand on me all the time she had me. I think she must have touched his arm or something to get a point across, and all I saw was his hand going up, like he was about to hit her. I never ran so fast in all my life. We almost tore her house apart. When we finished, she had called the police on him, and they were on their way. She kept telling him that he was going to jail, so he ran out of the house.

"I didn't see him again until her funeral when I was 20. He didn't even sit with the family. He just sat in the back and watched. When we went to the gravesite, I wanted to talk with him, but he sat in his car the whole time. When they put her in the ground, he drove off. Then when my mother died two years after that, I saw him again, and we talked. I told him that he was my brother and if there was anything he needed, just let me know. I was still in school, but Granny had left everything to me, and I was not really hurting for anything financially. He said that he would keep that in mind and, boy, did he. Periodically he would show up, sometimes with a girl, most of the time by himself, asking for money. I had so much guilt about him, so most of the time, I would give it to him.

"When I started working with Kyle, he would periodically give his bum friends my number for help. Then things looked like they were picking up for him. He was hanging around ball players and had good-looking women with him. I thought that he had finally found his way, but I was wrong. He was running some scams, and he sometimes needed my help to get out of them. Then one day, he brought Patrick in to us, and he has not really been back for money ever since that time. As a matter of fact, he doesn't even come to the office anymore."

I listened to him thinking that sounded like the Anthony I knew— someone that would hit his own grandmother. A scammer, a con man, a taker, yes, this person was the same man I had known. I thought, how could these two men be so different, and how could I have not seen the resemblance. That was the scariest part. Standing next to each other, they looked like twins. But night and day, that was who they were—night and day.

Finally, I said, "Did he ever tell you about any of the women he dated?"

"No, those poor ladies probably don't know what hit them."

I thought how true was that statement!

"No, we never got close enough to talk about anything like that."

There was so much I wanted to know, but I was afraid of what it might look like, me asking so many questions, and maybe he didn't

Illegal Love | 133

have the answers that I needed anyway, but one thing was sure—I had to tell him, and I had to tell him soon. We finished eating our pizza and then went home. All Robert could talk about now was when was I moving in. I didn't want to upset him, so I just said soon. That night, we slept, and as Robert's arms were wrapped around me, I drifted into a comfortable sleep.

When we got to work the next morning, Kyle was already there, and so was Tom. I looked through my workbasket and checked around my computer to see what I had missed. Kyle came by to see if I was feeling better, and I told him yes.

"If you need some time off, just let me know. We'll miss you, but we'd rather have you well."

"Thank you, Kyle."

Tom came by. He was so sympathetic. He just wanted to make sure that I was okay.

"I don't want to give you too much work today," he told me.

I reassured him that I was fine, and he could give me all the work he wanted. The day started like any other day. When the mail came, I got roses. I thought it was sweet. I figured Robert had sent them to try and cheer me up. I smelled them and smiled, thinking how sweet my baby was. As I held them, I read the card that was attached. It said, "No rose could ever compare to the beauty of you, and I hope that you feel better." I smiled and turned the card over. It said, "Love, Noel." When I jumped up, they tipped over, and the water went everywhere. Just then, Karan walked in.

"Are you all right?"

"Sure. Just knocked over this vase."

"You should be careful. You have some sensitive documents there."

I rolled my eyes. "I know."

She put a smirk on her face.

"I'm sorry that you got sick at the party. I hope it wasn't from meeting Etowah."

I stopped what I was doing. "No, it wasn't."

"Oh," she snickered, then went into her office. I knew that whatever was on the rumor mill had already started, and right now, I didn't care. I had bigger fish to fry. I couldn't mentally focus and get the scheduling right this morning, so when clients wanted to schedule an appointment, I had to transfer them to Karan. I told her that I still wasn't feeling well, but the truth was, my mind was elsewhere. I kept wondering when or if Noel was going to show his face again. Now that he knew where I was, it was just a matter of time.

It seemed everyone was having a very bad karmic day. Everything was going wrong that could. Even sweet Tom was in over his head. By the time lunch came, Robert was so wrapped up with a client he couldn't go. I didn't want to take the chance of going downstairs and probably hearing about what a spectacle I made of myself this weekend, so I just went to The Salad Tree across the street, but wouldn't you know it. There she was, sitting there in plain sight. Then she looked up and waved. I waved back as I looked up to the sky, asking God, *Why?* Against my better judgment, I went over to her table.

"Good afternoon, Niyokia."

"Hey, girl, get something and come and have a seat."

I went and picked up a salad and then sat down with her. She was almost finished, but I didn't think she was going to let something like that stop her.

"You know that I know about your engagement, so let me see the ring."

I held up my hand, and she gasped.

"It's the biggest diamond I've seen up close."

"Me too."

"How he did it?"

I told her about the Chinese restaurant and the cookies. She almost had tears in her eyes. I never would have thought her to be a romantic.

"That's typical Robert, to be so romantic and full of surprises. Everyone knows how nice he is."

"Yes, that's my Robert."

She smiled, ate some of her food, then said, "Speaking of your Robert ..."

"Yes?"

"When did you two actually start dating? You know, last year when I talked with you, you denied everything so vehemently that I took it at face value."

I thought even now she had to know everything.

"Niyokia, you don't take anything at face value. You probably didn't have any other sightings of us, so you just made some assumptions, right?"

Illegal Love | 135

"Okay, I'll go with that."

"It really was long after that."

"Oh. Well, since you're being open with me, I'll tell you this. You know that everyone thinks your little episode this weekend had something to do with his ex-girlfriend, but I don't."

"Really?"

"Oh yeah, but you see, I know things, and I know that you came to see me about a woman one day."

"Well, I was just curious."

"Yeah, we all are."

"Well, she didn't look like I thought she would, although she was beautiful."

"It's all a matter of opinion. Well, anyway, I know people, that's my business, and I say that you are too secure in your relationship with Robert to be worried about another woman, especially with this ring."

I just kept on eating.

"So, that means there was probably another man."

She caught me off guard, but I tried to keep my cool, so I continued to chew like she had said nothing, although I was about to choke.

"Well, you know that's just my opinion."

By then, she had finished her meal and got up to leave. "Stop by and see me again sometime. I'm not as bad as you think."

"I'll consider it."

With that, Niyokia walked across the street back into the building. At a time like this, I wished that I had someone to talk with, but there was no one but Robert and me, and I was not yet ready to come clean to him. I finished my meal and went back to the building. When I got back to the office, to my horror and surprise, Noel was there, sitting on one of the couches. I almost froze walking to my desk. He came over.

"Hey, it's Nikki, right?"

I looked around to see who could see us.

"Yeah."

He leaned close to the desk and whispered, "Did you get my flowers?"

"Yes, but you shouldn't have sent them."

"Why, I miss you and wanted you to know it. I have missed you, but I didn't know how to get in touch with you. Baby, I can explain everything."

"There's nothing to explain. You hurt me, and then almost got me sent to jail. Anthony, Noel, whatever your name is, I lost everything because of you."

"But if you would just give me a chance, things are going fine for me, and I can make it up to you."

"You could never make up for the marks on my back."

Just then, Kyle and Patrick came out of his office. Noel straightened up. He was pretending like he was asking me a question about my engagement. He turned to Patrick and Kyle.

"Robert has a lovely fiancée."

Then Kyle said, "Yes, and we have a lovely and wonderful person working with us."

They all walked towards the elevator, then Noel and Patrick left. Kyle went back to his office. Something deep down inside said *go talk to Robert now,* but the fear had me. I ran to the bathroom and threw water on my face. My heart was beating so rapidly, I could feel pain in my chest. I thought I was going to have a heart attack. To calm myself, I sat on a toilet and just breathed. In, out, in, out. I don't know how long I was in there, but I finally got myself under control. I went back to the office and started down the hall towards Robert's office, but just then, Tom came out of his office.

"Nikki, can—can I sp—speak with you for a moment?"

"Sure, Tom," and I walked down to his office. He closed the door as I came in. Both of us sat down.

"Is everything go—going okay with you?"

"Why do you ask that?"

"We—we—ll, I g—ga—gave you some documents earlier to—to—day and now—now they are all mes—messed up and I kn—kn—know that is not like you. I wanted to talk with yo—yo—you about it instead of going to Ky—Kyle or Karan."

"I'm sorry. I just have a lot on my mind today."

"Well yo—you know that you ca—can always talk to me."

"I know, Tom, thanks."

"No, re—re—really, you can talk to me."

When I looked at him, I really felt that I could. So I began my story from the beginning. Through my teary eyes, I could see the sympathy he had for me. When I finished, what I saw was pain for me, but not pity.

"You po—poor girl, you have be—been through hell."

He gave me a handkerchief.

"Dry yo—your eyes. I ha—have known Robert for a much lo—longer time than yo—you have, and I have to tell yo—you, he is as fair as they come. He will probably b—be upset, b—but not with you. Yo—you were the vi—victim in this whole si—situ—ation. Tell him be-before it's t—o—o late, and let him prove to yo—you he is the man you fell in lo—love with."

As I wiped my eyes, I knew that the words that had come from this sweet gentleman were true, and only truth could set me free. I told him that I would, but I needed to think on how I was going to tell Robert that the man from my past was his brother.

Tom said, "I have only met his bro—brother once or twice, and I never wo—would have thought that he was capable of doing something like that, but I did notice that he was an unscrupulous character. Let Go—God be your strength, and you will find the way."

As I got up to leave, Tom walked me to the door. I gave him a nice long hug.

"Thank you, again. You don't know what it feels like to be able to get this out and not be judged."

"It is not fo—for me to judge you, Nikki, nor is it for yo—you to judge yourself."

I went down to my desk to try to salvage the rest of the day. Driving home with Robert, I wanted to tell him, but I thought I should at least wait until we got to my place. When we got to my apartment, I told him to wait and I would go up to get some things for tomorrow. He said okay, and I got out the car. While walking up to my door, I wasn't feeling right. Once I got into my place, I had a bad vibe, but I just put it off to the pressures that I had been under all day. I put my things down, then something told me to check my answering machine. When I did, there was a message from Noel.

"You need to call me right away; it's important."

Reluctantly, I dialed the number he had left. The phone rang once.

"Hello."

"This is Nikki. How did you get my number?"

"You must have forgotten I have a way with people. The phone company is full of sympathetic women, and when someone is looking for his long lost sister because he is dying, well, if I would have tried any harder, I would have had her crying, and she would have given me your address too."

"You haven't changed."

"Yes, I have, and I have to talk with you."

He started in again.

"Noel, it's not going to work. I love Robert."

"You just don't remember how I made you feel, baby."

"Oh, I remember all right. I remember all of how you made me feel, and I have the scars to prove it."

"Now, don't go bringing that stuff up. I was having a bad time, but things are better now, and I can make it all up to you."

"You never will be able to do that—not in a million years."

When I said that, I must have angered him. Immediately, his tone changed. It was more brass and harsh sounding, the way that Anthony used to be. I got scared because I didn't know what to expect.

"I want to see you, and I think it would be in your best interest to come and see me."

"I don't think so. I'm going to tell Robert about us."

"I don't think that you will like *my* version of what happened to us."

"What do you mean?"

"Mine will have a little spice to it, and by the time I finish with you, you won't even have a job to go to."

"You can't do that; you can't lie about me."

"I can do whatever the hell I want to, and what I want right now is *you*."

The tears didn't come this time, not even with all the fear and pain I was feeling.

"What do you want?"

"That's better. I have a friend that lets me use his place sometimes, and I want you there tonight."

"I can't tonight."

"You keep forgetting who's in control here. I mean *tonight*."

"What do you want me there for?"

When I said it, I already knew. I wasn't completely stupid, even though recent and past events would suggest otherwise.

"All I want is a chance to show you that I've missed you. I need to show you that I can make you happy."

"Noel, I love Robert."

"You just think that because he's some kind of big-time lawyer. I want you here, or I'll make sure you lose him."

He gave me the address, and I hung up the phone. When I went back downstairs, I didn't have my things with me. I leaned on the driver side of the car, looked into those beautiful eyes of his—and lied.

"Baby, I have to run an errand, and then I'll come over later."

He kissed me gently as he always did and drove off. I went back upstairs, showered, and changed. I kept thinking it's not too late to call Robert and tell him the truth. I told myself that—all the way to the address Noel had given me. But then I thought, whose truth would he believe, mine or Noel's? After I parked, I thought I would throw up, but no such luck. Only panic and pain remained. As I walked up the stairs, the two flights seemed like the longest two flights I had ever climbed.

Chapter 12
From the Beginning

Blue lights, there were blue lights behind me. How long had I sat here? What time was it? A policeman came up to the car and flashed a light on me. He could see the tears coming down my face as I rolled down the window.

"Ma'am, are you all right?"

"Yes, sir."

"Well, I drove down the street and was gone for a while, and when I came back, you were still here. From the looks of things, you appear to be in distress. Is there something I can do?"

"Oh no, Officer. I'm sorry. Something got into my eye, and I pulled over to get it out. I am sorry."

"Okay, but next time, ma'am, try to get it out a little sooner. I wouldn't want anything to happen to you out in the night, alone like this."

"Yes, sir."

He went back to his car and drove away, and so did I. I couldn't believe that I was going to sleep with Noel after all that he had done to me. I was still going to sleep with him. I must be losing my mind. I drove to Robert's house all the while, trying to think of how I was going to tell him. When I got there, he was sitting on the sofa watching sports. He looked so innocent, and here I was, about to become another Etowah. I came and knelt down in front of him and turned off the TV.

140

Illegal Love | 141

"Baby, we were winning."

"I need to talk to you."

"Okay. Is everything all right?"

I heard the concern in his voice, and it broke my heart to know I was about to break his.

"No, not really."

"This sounds serious."

"It is."

I leaned up and kissed him gently on the lips. Maybe this would be the last time I could do this, and I wanted to remember the sweet smell of his breath and the softness of his lips.

"What I'm about to tell you will change the way you think of me, and when I finish, you might not want to marry me."

He sat straight up.

"You might not even want me working for the firm anymore either."

I could see his body tense up. I lowered my head and closed my eyes as I began.

"Remember when I told you about my past?"

"Yes."

"And remember the guy I told you who had put me in that situation and had beaten me up so badly?"

"Yes."

"Well, he's in town."

"And?"

"And you know him."

He looked puzzled.

"How could I know him?"

I hesitated for a moment, then looked up into those wonderful, loving brown eyes.

"It's Noel."

"What's Noel?"

He repeated the name back to me almost comic-like.

"My Anthony and your Noel is the same person."

"Are you sure?"

The look of disbelief was all over his face. He was hurt and there was nothing I could do.

"Positive."

I told him about the first party I went to at Patrick's house. "That was why I got so drunk that night. I saw him there. Then when we were at the party last week, I didn't get sick because of Etowah. He saw me and had me cornered. Then you came and said that he was your brother, and I didn't know what to do."

I blurted it all out as he stood up.

"Why didn't you tell me then?"

"I was afraid."

"Of *me*? You know that I would never hurt you."

"He's your brother. I didn't know if you would choose me over him."

"Okay, I can see how that would cross your mind in the beginning, but then, even after I told you of our estranged relationship?"

"Well, by then, I was ashamed for not telling you sooner."

He paced back and forth, putting his hands on his head and sometimes on his sides.

"Nikki, how do you expect to marry someone if you don't trust them?"

"I do trust you. It was me I had lost the trust in. I didn't think that you could love me because of my stupid mistakes."

"Nikki, I told you before when I put that ring on your finger that I loved you unconditionally."

"I know, I just didn't believe in myself."

I was about to tell him the rest, but he grabbed his jacket and stormed out of the door. I ran after him, calling his name, but when I got outside, he was already gone. I waited there for hours, scared. I didn't know what to think. Maybe I should call someone, but I didn't know who to call. Not even Tom could help me now. Maybe he just took a drive to get away and think, or maybe he went after Noel. My God, what have I done? I finally cried myself to sleep on the sofa waiting for him. I think the VCR read 3:45 when I heard the door open. I jumped up.

"Robert?"

"Yes, it's me."

He came over to the sofa where I had been lying and sat next to me.

"Where have you been?"

Illegal Love | 143

"At first, I just needed to get away, but then I kept seeing your back and flashes of him beating you kept going through my mind. So I went to Patrick's."

My heart stopped, and I sat up. *I knew it.*

"You didn't hurt him, did you?"

What had he found out? Did Noel tell him about us tonight? I was frightened, but I had to hear it.

"Patrick showed me to his room in the guesthouse, but he wasn't there, so I waited. When he got there, I just grabbed him. It was like the time I thought that he was going to hit Granny. I just snapped. I was so mad I could have killed him."

I grabbed his arm.

"Robert, you didn't hurt him, did you?"

He didn't answer me; he just continued talking.

"I just started slapping him around. He never really got his balance, and then I threw him on the ground. As I was getting ready to pounce on him, he said, 'I'm sorry, man, I'm sorry.'

"I asked him how he could do that to another human being, especially a woman. Noel just looked confused at first, then he wanted to know what I was talking about. I said you know damn well what I'm talking about—the way you beat Nikki. I asked him if he had seen the damage and scars he had left on you.

"Baby, then he started getting up, but I wasn't having it. I jumped at him, and he stayed there. Noel went on about how he was a different person back then, running scams and with the frustration of possibly going to jail, he said he just took it out on you. He said that you didn't deserve any of it. I told him damned right, no one did. Noel kept apologizing and said, 'You really love her, don't you?' He said, 'I promise you, I have never hurt anyone else like that before in my life.'

"I still wanted to kick him or something, just to let him feel part of the pain he must have put you through. Instead, I just sat down on the nearest chair and watched him getting up from the floor. I couldn't—I just couldn't believe my own brother would do something like this to someone. I had envisioned a monster doing that to you, but now to find out that monster was my own flesh and blood. I told Noel that there was nothing left between us anymore. I told him we were no longer brothers. I told him that I had always hoped that he wanted something more out of life, something better than the life he had led, but now I know better. Baby, that's when I walked out and came home."

I put my arms around him and held him. I said, "I'm so sorry."

He held me tightly.

"No, I'm the one who should be sorry."

"You had no way of knowing your brother was capable of doing something like this."

"Yes, but I shouldn't have judged you when you told me. I can live with your reasons if you can live with me doubting you."

"I love you."

And we stayed there on the sofa 'til dawn. When morning came, Robert called in for both of us. We just stayed together all day, being with one another. It was different than any other time we had ever spent together, and it was a weird sort of peacefulness.

For the rest of the week, things with us were wonderful and work was fine. I even went to Tom and told him that everything had worked out, and he was happy for me. Robert had been really pressing me to move all week, and by the weekend, I had called Mr. Robins to let him know of my plans to vacate the apartment. He let me know that there would be no problem with it, and that there would be no early termination fees or anything.

Robert and I spent the weekend packing up my apartment. We moved a lot of the small things. Next week, we were going to find someone to give my furniture to. It had served me well, and now, maybe it could help someone less fortunate than myself.

On Monday morning, work seemed better; life seemed better. I still had my doubts about Noel. He could, at any moment, come and blow me out of the water. I knew that he had not told Robert about that night, and I hadn't told him either. There was always that lingering possibility that he would ruin it for me and Robert, but so far, so good. I figured that one day this could all change, but for right now, I would just try to be happy for the moment.

By Tuesday morning, everything was back to normal. Robert and I drove into work together. We kissed each other before he went into his office. I checked the messages and transferred everything accordingly. When mail came, I sorted it then distributed it the way that is was supposed to be. When it was time to go to lunch, Robert could not go. I went downstairs to the cafeteria. There was Niyokia sitting alone. She hadn't seen me yet, but I decided to stop anyway.

"Are you expecting anyone?"

"No, go ahead and have a seat."

I sat down, blessed my food, and started eating. She didn't say anything right away. I hadn't sat down with her for gossip. I just thought it would be nice for us both not to have lunch alone. Finally, she said, "I really shouldn't be telling you this."

I interrupted her by saying, "Well, then, don't."

"Yeah, but you know me. Y'all will be losing two of your people soon."

I stopped eating.

"Yeah, it seems Karan and Joel are moving up to the top floor."

I still said nothing. Finally, I started back eating.

"Do you want to know why or not?"

I still said nothing. She rolled her eyes and continued. "It seems Karan feels her position there is no longer needed since a certain *someone* has been there. She feels everyone is putting their trust in the receptionist more than they do in the office manager. And you know wherever Karan goes, Joel goes."

"Really?"

"Oh, yes. Before they came to Kyle, they were with this other guy. I can't remember his name, but he was down the street. That's how I met Karan. She didn't know the area very well and one day we met while having lunch. After a while, Kyle moved down to the 10th floor from the 20th floor, and he was having a hard time keeping a receptionist. So I told him about Karan. Shortly after, she came, and Joel was right behind her."

I thought how that made sense. They seemed somehow to be joined at the hip. I continued eating my salad until she said, "And you know what that means for you, don't you?"

"No, what?"

"They're going to need someone to take her place."

That didn't occur to me. I just assumed that Kyle would hire someone else for the position. I told her that too. She looked at me as if she wasn't sure to believe me or not, but said nothing about it. Then she looked at the wristwatch.

"Damn! I've been down here too long. Wait and see if what I told you happens."

Then she got up and left. I sat there for just a few moments before going upstairs. Karan was bopping around like she thought no one would know about her plans. I went to Robert's office to talk with him. He let me sit down before he asked what was going on.

I told him what I had heard and wanted to know if I should talk with Kyle about it. He said that it might only be a rumor, and if that were so, then I would get them into trouble, but on the other hand, if it wasn't, then yes, it was best that he knew about it. I decided to talk with Kyle.

I went past my desk, down towards Kyle's office, knocked on the door, and waited.

"Come in."

As I did, I closed the door.

"Nikki, what do I owe this pleasure?"

"Well, I'm not sure how to handle a situation."

He put his elbows on his desk and rested his head in his hands. "Well, let's talk about it."

"I have come across some information that could be hurtful if it is incorrect, but if it is correct, I think that the person it is being done to should know about it."

"I see."

"Yes, and I'm a little torn."

"It's simple to me. Where do your loyalties lie?"

"Oh, well, then, *that's* easy. Karan and Joel are getting jobs with Bailey, Bird, and Banks on the 20th floor."

He sat up and leaned back in his seat. "And how do you know this?"

"Niyokia from the 6th floor told me today."

"Well, you know that I don't take to gossip from others."

"I know, but we all know that if there is anything about anything going on in this building, then she knows about it. I just wanted to pass on what I knew because I think if it is true, this is a poor way for them to show you how much they appreciate what you have done for them over the years. On top of that, they might be trying to take some clients with them."

"Well, yes, you are right, but again, I do not subscribe to gossip. So I think I'll just call upstairs myself."

"Okay."

I got up to leave the room, but before I walked out the door, he said, "I'll need to talk with you later if this is true."

"Okay."

I went back down to Robert's office. When I got there, Robert said, "What did he say?"

"He said he did not subscribe to gossip, and that he was going to make a call for himself."

"Yeah, because most of the gossip around this building usually has something to do with him."

I started laughing and confessed, "Yeah, I've probably been in on some of that."

"Well, sure. You did go to lunch with him a couple of times and let him take you home, right?"

"Robert, you're not jealous about that, are you?"

"No, I got over that a long time ago, but in the beginning, it did look pretty suspicious, and he usually gets his way with the ladies."

"Well, I have never been interested in him, at least not when I found out he was married. Robert, can I ask you a question?"

"Anything, my darling."

"That night at Patrick's party, what did George say about Etowah?"

"Oh, that?" He got up from his chair and strolled over to the window. I loved it when he stared out into the vastness of the earth. It gave him such a dignified look.

"I asked him how he could let Buffy bring her to the party, knowing that I was bringing you."

"Okay and ...?"

"George said he had not thought of that, but he brought her because Buffy had been telling her about Patrick and Etowah wanted to meet him. You see, she has a thing for men with money, and since her boss's wife found out about them, she has been demoted from her position, and he has cut her off. So now she's looking for her next victim."

I went over to his side of the room and hugged him from behind. Then we walked over to his desk.

"Now, aren't you glad that things didn't work out between you two?"

"Of course, my darling."

"You sure know how to suck up really well."

As he sat down, Robert reached up, pulled me around to where he was, and gave me a great big kiss. I was snug in his lap when Kyle knocked on the door, so I quickly jumped up when he came into the room.

"Oh, good, I was just looking for you, Nikki."

"I'm sorry, I just came in to ask Robert a question."

"That's all right, I wasn't questioning you. I just got off the telephone with Mr. Banks. You were right. Nikki, you may not know this, but I used to work for Bailey, Bird, and Banks."

"No, I didn't know that."

"Yes, and we still have great respect for each other. When I decided I wanted to start my own firm, they were more than helpful. That's why it's important that you don't burn your bridges; never burn your bridges behind you. Well, that's all I have to say, except thanks for the information."

After he left, I told Robert that I would see him later and returned to my desk. When I got there, Kyle buzzed me and asked me to have Karan and Joel come to his office immediately. I did as I was told.

Karan came out with her usual look of *What does he want know* this *time?* And me, with my usual *I don't know* expression. She walked down the hall to Kyle's office. Soon, Joel came out his room and closed the door once he entered the boss's room. They were in there for a long time, then one after the other, they burst out of his office. Karan was screaming.

"Good riddance to you all! I was tired of working for pennies anyway! I'm about to embark on a new journey. You all will still be stuck here, and I'm on my way to a better place."

Joel said nothing as he walked down to her office with his box in hand. It was like he had already started packing a while ago. Karan was still yelling something as she was gathering her things. Joel walked over to the lobby area, sat on the couch, and looked at me. Finally, he said, "You had something to do with this, didn't you?"

I acted as if I didn't hear him. Karan was still carrying on like a mad woman.

"You'll find out it's not all what you think it is here. None of you will be able to function without us."

Just then, Karan came out of the office and gave me the most evil look, then they walked over to the elevator and got on. Kyle called me after a while and asked if they had left.

"Yes."

Then he asked me down to his office. After I sat down, he began. "I'm pleased with your work, and I probably would have fired Karan eventually anyway."

Illegal Love | 149

I said nothing.

"Now that we have an office manager's position available, I think that you're the most qualified person to run the office."

My eyes got big. I had this big grin on my face, but words eluded me.

"Is that all you can say?"

"Oh, thank you, Kyle."

"You *do* know how to do the things that Karan was doing, don't you?"

"Yes, sir."

"I thought so, but for a moment there, I didn't seem to think that you wanted to jump into it."

"Oh, yes, I do, sir."

"Well, as soon as you get her office cleaned out and get everything transferred back to your new area, call a temp agency to get us a receptionist."

I thanked him, then ran down the hall like a schoolgirl. I didn't even knock on Robert's door, I just threw it open.

"You got it, didn't you?"

I ran to his arms.

"Yes!"

"I'm so proud of you."

I was too thrilled. It took me the rest of the week to get her things out and mine in. On Friday, I called her answering machine to say that she could come in to pick up the rest of her belongings at any time down at the security desk in the lobby of the building. Next, I called The Right Person's Temp Agency and confirmed that a new temp would start on Monday.

When we got home that night, there was a message on the answering machine for Robert from Patrick. He called him back and when he got off the phone, he said, "Noel's in jail."

"What for?"

"Patrick says it's attempted murder."

"What?"

"Patrick says that one of Noel's girlfriends came over to see him and for some reason they got into an argument, he thinks. All he really knows is that Noel ran up to the house saying he was sorry and to call an ambulance. He said when the ambulance got there, they called the police. He had beaten the girl unconscious."

I sat down; the memories of my beatings seemed fresh in my mind now. I thought about that poor girl.

"What are you going to do?"

"Will you go with me to see him?"

I didn't want to, but this was my soon-to-be husband's brother and my ex-lover.

"Yes."

When we got to the jail, they allowed us to see him. Robert asked him what happened. Noel said, "I'm not really sure. We were drinking, and I asked her to get me some more and she said no, that she was not Patrick, and she wasn't going to run every time I said run. I don't know what happened after I picked up this stick I had in the house. I just hit her once, at least that's all I remember."

Robert looked at his brother with disgust and pity. Finally, he said, "Noel, they say she had been hit 44 times."

"I don't remember it; I honestly don't remember hitting her that many times."

I looked at him sitting there in front of us, looking sorry for what he had done and I wanted to believe him, but I couldn't. I knew that Robert wanted to believe him, just for his sanity. I wondered if Noel remembered hitting me all the times that he did it.

"I can get you counsel, but I won't be your lawyer."

"Please, if you get me out, I promise I won't do this again."

Robert stood up, and as we were leaving the room, he said. "Noel, if you get out of this mess, I don't want to ever hear from you again."

We left the room and nothing further was said. I had expected Noel to say something about us, but he didn't. I held tightly to Robert's arm as we left. I could tell this was one of the hardest things he must have ever done in his life. It wasn't Noel's style to beg, and I knew that we would never hear from him again. Even to the end, he had to be the one in control. I was amazed that he let me go, but he said nothing. Maybe he really did care for me some, or maybe he really did love his brother.

On the drive home, Robert said, "He swore to me he would not hurt another person."

I put my hand on his. "Baby, it's not your fault. He promised me after each time that he beat me that he would not hurt me again either."

It was the first time I had seen Robert cry, and I felt so sorry for him. As much as I felt I had been through, I knew he had gone through a lot also and survived his own pain. That weekend we packed up the rest of my things, moved a lot of my stuff into his apartment, and moved my old furniture into storage. I had not found anyone to give it to, so I'd keep it until I found the right person.

On Monday, we got to the office and found the new receptionist was downstairs waiting at the security desk. As we rode the elevator up together, I sized her up. She was meek-looking, wore glasses, and her hair was in a tight bun. She looked younger than me, but lacked the experience I had at her age. I introduced Robert to her. She had introduced herself as Patsy Cadawall. She seemed more frightened than I was on my first day but just as eager to work. I showed her to her desk and then to my office. After everyone had come to work, I took her around to meet them. We spent most of the morning practicing on the phone system. I showed her how to transfer the calls to all the guys. I let her know if she had any questions at all, she could come to me. I had to take some things down to George's office, and as I was passing the front desk, there was Kyle, leaning over towards Patsy, and I heard the same old lines he used on me.

"Patsy, you don't have to call me sir. I'm Kyle, and if any of the other associates ask you to call them sir, just let me know."

Then I heard him mention lunch. I smiled and shook my head as I went down to George's office. On the way back towards my office, I stopped by Patsy's desk since Kyle was no longer there.

"Is everything okay?"

"Yes, ma'am, but Mr. Simmons, I mean, Kyle, just asked me to lunch."

"Sweetie, come with me."

I took her to the ladies' room down the hall and said, "Have a seat."

She looked around and only saw toilets.

"That'll do just fine. First, Tom is married, and he would be too scared to ask you out anyways. Second, George is just a big loveable bear, but he's engaged to Buffy, and they're expecting their first child any day now. Third, Robert's mine. He's totally off limits."

I showed her the rock.

"Fourth, but not the least, is Kyle. He's totally gorgeous and totally owns the place, but he's totally married."

"Wow! How long have you been here?"

"A little over 2 years, but I started out just like you."

The look on her face seemed familiar, and I thought later on I'd ask her if she needed some well-loved furniture.

About the Author

Felicia Truttier is a native of Atlanta, Georgia. Her love of writing began in high school, where she and a friend traded journals for Christmas gifts. Later, she realized that writing short stories was more fulfilling. As she began to share her stories with family, friends and co-workers the rave reviews encouraged her to write even more, but just enough to keep them curious about her fascinating characters.

The writing that had began as a hobby first became therapeutic and has now blossomed into her passion... Felecia is encouraged by her heroines as they overcome hard times to see clear days. As they have been to her, Felecia hopes that they will be an encouragement to everyone to show that hard times don't always last. As her characters have shown, there is a light at the end of every tunnel and all you have to do is walk towards it.

CPSIA information can be obtained at www.ICGtesting.com
Printed in the USA
266341BV00003B/143/P